Black Friday  Volume 1

Black Friday Volume 1

Noah AJ Wright

www.urbanbooks.net

Urban Books, LLC
78 East Industry Court
Deer Park, NY 11729

Black Friday Volume 1 ©copyright 2010 Noah AJ Wright

ISBN 13: 978-1-60162-267-9
ISBN 10: 1-60162-267-8

First Printing April 2010
Printed in the United States of America

10 9 8 7 6 5 4 3 2 1

Distributed by Kensington Publishing Corp.
Submit Wholesale Orders to:
Kensington Publishing Corp.
C/O Penguin Group (USA) Inc.
Attention: Order Processing
405 Murray Hill Parkway
East Rutherford, NJ 07073-2316
Phone: 1-800-526-0275
Fax: 1-800-227-9604

Prologue

Kasheef's heart felt as if it would explode as he sat in the federal courtroom. News cameras were littered throughout while both supporters and the opposition awaited the verdict. It was the day that he would meet his fate, the day that the rest of his days would be determined by the decision that the jury rendered. On the outside Kasheef was calm and collected. His chocolate Armani suit rested perfectly against his dark skin and medium athletic build. With his hair cut neatly in a fresh Caesar and his eyes filled with sincerity, one would never guess that the man sitting before them was a drug kingpin. A distinguished business man, yes, but a drug kingpin, no. Kasheef scanned the jury with his eyes and couldn't read their expressions. He didn't know what tomorrow held for him and for the first time in his life he was afraid. Prison was not an option for him. To lock him up would be equivalent to stealing his pride, and he refused to live on his knees. Being told when to eat, sleep, how frequently he could use the phone, and monitoring who he interacted with was not an appealing lifestyle for him. The harsh reality of being locked up was not for him. The life and times of an inmate wasn't for him. Kasheef hoped and prayed that the verdict would be delivered in his favor, because if it wasn't he was already prepared to go out in a blaze of glory. A $10,000 cash payment to one of the assigned court officers ensured that he would have his weapon of choice, a chrome .45, taped underneath the defense table. He discreetly ran his hand along the underside of the cherry wood and felt the cold steel that was strapped securely in place. It was his insurance policy.

Kasheef was not green to the game. He had been in the dope game since he was a young boy, so he knew that his day of judgment was inevitable. While many glamorized the street life, he knew the real deal and was well aware that his reign could end in only one of two ways: prison or death. He would much rather hold court in the streets for his actions, in his own environment, where he would at least have a chance to survive. Sitting in a courtroom made him a sitting duck. He knew that it was very possible that the jury would convict him, and that the judge would throw the book at him, sending him away for the remainder of his natural life. He turned and stared into the eyes of Norelle, his girlfriend, who greeted him with a wink and a sexy smirk. Cameras flashed continuously in her face, but she took it all in stride. She knew that they had recognized her face from her very public arrest that had occurred the day before. Almost as soon as she was handcuffed, she was released. Bail money was not an issue. Now she sat silently with her fingers crossed as she awaited Kasheef's verdict. Norelle's own legal troubles were nonexistent at the moment. The only thing that mattered to her was what was going on right now. Kasheef had to admit that Norelle was a beautiful girl. From her Manolo stilettos to her Marc Jacobs two-piece suit with matching clutch, she represented all that he was. He had taken her from the gutter and put her on a throne beside his own as the queen of the streets. She held her title well, and indeed commanded attention like royalty. *You didn't think I would come,* she mouthed.

"All rise!" the bailiff announced loudly, causing Kasheef to turn back around in his chair. "The honorable Judge Campbell Martin presiding."

"Be seated," the judge mumbled as he took his own behind the large pedestal. "Has the jury reached a verdict?"

The face of the foreman told Kasheef all that he needed to know. Kasheef gripped the steel underneath the table and took a deep breath as he prepared himself for what was about to go down.

"Yes, we have, Your Honor."

"And what say you?" the judge inquired.

"We the jury . . ."

Kasheef's hand wrapped tightly around the gun.

"Find the defendant . . . ."

His heart beat in his ears, blocking out all sound, as he watched the foreman's lips mouth the words.

Pow! Pow! Pow!

The verdict fell on deaf ears as the courtroom erupted in mayhem.

Chapter One

Norelle looked at the clock. The more time that passed, the more irritated she became. It was already one in the morning and Kasheef still hadn't come home. She folded the clothes that she had spread out on her bed and packed them neatly inside her Louis Vuitton tote. *This nigga knows we've got to catch a plane tomorrow morning. He should've been back. He's so unreliable. All I need is one weekend. One weekend when it is just about me. He can't even give me that.*

She was anxious for her sorority reunion. It had been six years since she'd seen any of her sorority sisters, and when she'd gotten the invitation to go on a reunion cruise with them, she was ecstatic. She knew that everyone would be there, along with their significant others, so she made sure she told Kasheef way in advance so that he could put her on his schedule.

Having a man as fine as Kasheef was a plus. His dark, prominent features, sleepy bedroom eyes, and amazing physique were every woman's fantasy. He was even taller than she was, which was definitely a perk. Usually most men who had been blessed with his type of features had also been cursed financially. Fine men were always the maintenance men, or the construction workers you admired in passing. Kasheef, however, was the total package. He had pockets as deep as the Pacific Ocean and he was willing to fulfill all of her material desires. This in itself gave her bragging rights. His looks and charm, along with the many diamonds he had blessed her with, were sure to make her the envy of all of her old friends. Not to mention the semi-successful modeling career she'd had.

There was one person in particular she was excited about running into: her best friend, Carmen. They were close, and Carmen had been like a sister to her during their time at Spelman. Like so many others they had promised to never lose touch after graduation, but life interjected and intimate conversations every day became occasional courtesy calls. She couldn't wait to see her and she couldn't wait for Carmen to meet Kasheef. He wasn't perfect, but he was hers, and Norelle couldn't wait to show him off. *If the nigga make it,* she thought angrily as she watched the clock strike 1:30 A.M.. *He's not even packed yet.* Norelle pulled his suitcase out of the closet and tossed it onto the bed, then threw his underwear and socks inside. She was trying to give Kasheef the benefit of the doubt, but once 2:00 A.M. found her bed still empty she couldn't help but pick up the phone. *He better answer my call.*

***

"Why'd you want to meet in Queens? We always do business at your spot in Long Island," Mizan slurred as he stared around the crowded night club and shifted uncomfortably in his seat. The atmosphere was loud and boisterous. It was definitely not the environment to be talking money in. The club was popping as young men and women entered, dressed in their best attire.

Kasheef looked at the man in front of him, studying him intensely for a few seconds before he replied, "I felt like switching things up. This is my club. Wires can't pick up a signal in here."

"What you think I'm wired up, fam?"

"I don't know, *fam* . . . are you?" Kasheef responded as he stared Mizan directly in the eyes, trying to sense any form of deception. He was not the type to play games or beat around the bush. If he had suspicions about a person he put them on the table. It was important for him to have thorough people around him. Real men respected his bluntness, because they knew the game and followed the same rules that he did.

"Yo', Sheef, you ill'n right now, son. I've been copping my weight from you for years, fam, don't insult me," Mizan stated seriously.

Kasheef had done business with Mizan for the past two years and they had never encountered any problems. Mizan always had his money on time and it was always on point. He knew that he was wrong for doubting his man, but Kasheef would rather be safe than sorry. In this game there wasn't any room for error. Mizan had caught a little one year bid behind an illegal gun charge, and Kasheef thought that it was a bit odd that upon his release Mizan was back in the streets full force, attempting to cop his normal order of forty bricks. Kasheef would have preferred for Mizan to be more cautious and lay low for a couple months before dilving back into the game, but he was a grown man and Kasheef wasn't into schooling niggas. He kept to himself so that his name would never pop out on federal radar. He had to make sure Mizan had not switched sides.

"You're right, fam, I'm on some other shit. You know with all these niggas bumping they gums like bitches you can't be too careful," Kasheef said hesitantly as he relaxed some. He leaned back in the booth with his shot glass extended in the air.

"No doubt," Mizan responded with a half smile. He raised his glass as well and tapped it against Kasheef's. "Now that you got your panties out of a bunch . . . about this business—"

The ringing of the Kasheef's phone stopped Mizan in

mid-sentence. Kasheef looked at the caller ID, noticing it was Norelle. He put up his finger to signal for Mizan to put his conversation on hold and then picked up the call. "What's good?"

"You tell me, Sheef. I thought you would be home by now," Norelle stated. She tried to keep her tone in check because she knew that Kasheef did not appreciate disrespect, but even in her best attempt her attitude was apparent. *This nigga want a whole lot of respect for somebody who keeps playing me to the left. When he starts keeping respectful hours maybe I'll hold my tongue a little bit more.*

"I'm handling this business right now. I'll be there," he replied vaguely.

"Babe, you know we have to catch a plane tomorrow. You're not even packed." Her voice went from angry to desperate. Norelle was high maintenance and a very dependent woman. She hated to be kept waiting. It made her feel unimportant.

"Yeah, I said I'll be there. Give me a minute," he stated in a disengaged tone.

Kasheef smirked as he watched Mizan pull the arm of a young woman passing by their table. He peeped her from head to toe and licked his lips as his eyes focused on her apple-shaped behind.

"Sheef?" Norelle whined into the phone, knowing he wasn't paying attention to her.

"I'm here," he answered in irritation, and focused his attention back on his call.

"Where are you anyway? You in the club?" she asked heatedly.

Unwilling to hear her bitching, he ended the call quickly. "Don't wait up, ma. I'll be there after I handle this business. Don't worry about your reunion. I'll be packed and ready by the time you wake up." Before she could protest he put the dial tone to her ear and closed his cell.

Mizan was kicking game to his company so Kasheef decided to lay low and let his man enjoy his freedom. He called one of the waitresses over and ordered a round of drinks.

"What you drinking on, ma?" Kasheef asked the girl that Mizan was with.

"Call me Alija," she said with a dazzling smile. Her golden, soft M•A•C lip gloss glistened and her perfectly straight teeth were enticing to Kasheef. The fact that she looked him directly in the eye was a turn on for him. She wasn't shy and had the confidence of a supermodel.

"Okay, Alija, what you drinking?" he repeated as he returned her stare. He had to admit the girl was gorgeous. Her almond-colored skin and jet black hair complimented her chinky hazel eyes. Her body was flawless in the Juicy Couture she was rocking. She was dressed casually, yet he still found her sexy. She did not have to show it all in order to catch his eye. He was attracted to and curious about the hidden treasure that lay beneath the expensive fabric of her clothes. He had to remind himself of the real woman he had at home in Norelle just to break his stare. He allowed Mizan to chill out and kept the drinks coming all night, to show his boy a good homecoming. He made sure that he didn't get too tipsy, remembering the business that was still left unattended. The night came to a close around four in the morning as the partygoers began to vacate the club.

"It was nice to meet you both. I had a good time," Alija said as she stood up from the table. "Call me," she said to Mizan. She gave him a sexy wink before she left. Kasheef could not stop his eyes from following her backside as she sashayed away from the table.

Kasheef and Mizan waited until the club cleared out before they ascended the steps to the loft office above. "I see you doing you again," Kasheef stated as he sat down in his leather office chair.

Mizan laughed drunkenly and wobbled a little bit as he approached a chair.

"You good, baby?" Kasheef asked, noticing Mizan's lack of balance.

"I'm a'ight, baby boy. I'm good . . . Trying to get this money, nah mean?" Mizan replied a little too loudly.

Kasheef felt his phone vibrate and he picked it up, noticing Norelle's name on the ID. He sent her to voicemail and sighed. The fact that she wasn't asleep let him know that she was up just waiting for him to walk through the door. He knew that there would be hell to pay when he arrived home. The longer he stayed out, the higher Norelle's temperature would rise. When he finally did step foot inside their door, she would be ready to blow. He shook his head in regret because he knew that he was only adding fuel to the fire by ignoring her call. He needed to wrap his business up so that he could hurry to the crib. He didn't want beef with Norelle because he knew that it would take a couple of shopping sprees to make her happy again. It was in his best interest to wrap up the night. It would save him a couple thousand dollars in the end.

**

Alija walked through the crowd in the parking lot as she made her way to her car. Her girls had all found men to kick it with after the club, but she was exhausted and also had a child to go home to. She switched her way to the car and stopped midway once she realized she'd forgotten her clutch purse. She'd set it down when she was entertaining Mizan and Kasheef.

"Damn it!" she yelled as she took off her stiletto pumps. She held them in her hand as she went back into the club. It was completely empty when she stepped inside, so she quickly made her way back to the table. "Okay, where is my purse?" she mumbled tiredly. "Damn it!" Noticing that a light was shining from the second level, she made her way upstairs to see who was still in the club. She hoped that there was a manager still working so that she could see if someone had turned her belongings in. Unaware of what she was stepping into, she peeked her head around the corner and into the room.

***

"So how many you need?" Kasheef asked Mizan as he walked to his wall safe and began to put in the combination.

Mizan stood up on wobbly legs. "Yo', fam, it was jumping in this mu'fucka tonight," he said in slurred speech. As he spoke he stepped closer to Kasheef. Kasheef noticed his man was wild'n. Mizan had never been the boisterous, showboating type, but tonight he was in rare form. He dismissed Mizan's unusual behavior. He knew that Mizan had been locked up for a year. If you added that with being a little twisted from the nonstop flow of liquor, it was understandable how Mizan could be acting out of his usual calm demeanor.

Kasheef laughed lightly and opened the safe. "I hear you, fam. How many you want though? Let's finish this so I can break out." When he turned around he was staring down the barrel of a 9 mm.

"All of 'em! Clear that mu'fuckin' safe out, nigga!" Mizan yelled, perfectly coherent, as he pressed the pistol to Kasheef's dome at point-blank range.

Kasheef's blood boiled as he ice grilled the man before him. He instantly regretted that he hadn't followed his first mind. "I see you sobered up," he remarked with venom.

"I see you slipping, fam. Don't take this personally though, baby. It's all in the game, nigga, so just be easy and empty out that safe."

Kasheef nodded and reached into the safe. He began removing bricks of heroin slowly, one by one. "You had to do it like this, fam?" Kasheef said without emotion, vying for time as he frantically put the clip in the unloaded gun inside his safe. He knew that it was almost impossible to do with one hand, and when Mizan clocked him upside his temple with his weapon, he knew that he was close to death.

"You think I'm stupid, fam?" Mizan yelled as he cocked his gun and fired a warning shot into the air. "Let me see them hands!"

Kasheef heard someone gasp at the door, and when Mizan averted his eyes, Kasheef took his shot. In one swift motion he reached inside the safe, loaded his pistol, and blasted off without hesitation.

*****

Boom!

The blast from the gun resounded loudly throughout the building, bouncing from wall to wall until it met with Alija's ears. Shocked and in terror, her eyes grew big as she silently regretted witnessing something that she was never meant to see. Her eyes met Kasheef's. She stared at him; he stared at her.I In distress they both waited to gauge the other's reaction.

Run, Alija! Move before this nigga kills you too!

When the words finally registered in her brain, Alija took off. Instinctively, she quickly descended the steps two at a time. The gunshot had been so loud that it felt like bells were going off in her ears. "Oh, shit . . . oh, shit," she whispered as she felt herself becoming nauseated. Vomit tickled the back of her throat as she tried her hardest to hold it down before it erupted.

"Yo'!" Kasheef yelled after her as he ran up on her and grabbed her elbow. She fought him viciously, slapping and kicking for her life.

"No! Let me go! You killed him!" she gasped as she tried her hardest to free herself from his hold. "Please . . . please, I won't tell. I swear to God!" Their struggle ensued, but when

Alija finally snatched her arm away from him she lost her bearings. The long fall down the remainder of the stairs introduced her face to the hard cement floor. She felt the pain that echoed throughout her limbs, but she couldn't afford to let it slow her down. Frantically, she attempted to stand. Before she could get off of the ground, Kasheef had descended the steps and blocked her path to safety.

"Calm the fuck down!" he growled menacingly as he grabbed her by both shoulders and shook her until she was quiet.

"Oh my God. You killed him," she whispered as she doubled over crying. She was unable to silence herself, but afraid of the retribution for making so much noise.

"Listen," he said through closed teeth as he grabbed her chin. His gaze penetrated through her and she could see her impending death in his eyes. "You ain't see shit, you don't know shit, nah mean?"

She nodded. With her fear controlling her reflexes, she shook violently as she cried uncontrollably. She was unable to stop the sobs that were spilling out of her, but she tried desperately, afraid that if she did not be quiet, Kasheef would surely murder her where she stood.

"Go home . . . and keep your fucking mouth shut, you heard?"

She raised her shaking hands in front of her defensively and replied, "Thank you. I swear I won't say anything."

Kasheef watched her walk out of the club. He knew that he had broken the number one rule and that was to never ever leave any witnesses, but something in him held him back from taking the young girl's life. He did not like that he could put so much fear in a person. Guilt overcame him in that split second. The look of terror on the girl's face frightened even Kasheef. He was afraid of the amount of power he held. He felt inhumane and sometimes resented the cruelty and suffering he had inflicted in the streets. He watched as Alija sped off recklessly from the scene and then placed a call to some of his goons. He needed to get the body out of his office and he needed to do it quick.

***

Alija rushed into her two-bedroom apartment and made sure she locked the deadbolt behind her. "Oh my God! What just happened? What in the fuck just happened?" she repeated over and over again as she paced back and forth over the hardwood floor. "How did I get myself into this?" she asked herself as tears fell from her eyes. She could not get the scene out of her head. The blood, so much blood, and the deafening blast of the gunshot that resonated in her ears. Each time she closed her eyes all she saw was the red flow of blood as if left Mizan's body. She felt like she could not breathe, and her hands felt dirty. She snatched her shirt off and rubbed her bare skin to calm rising goose bumps. She ran into the bathroom, kicking off the rest of her clothes on the way, and jumped into the shower, not even waiting for the water to heat up. She scrubbed her skin roughly, as if she could cleanse her soul of the sin she'd just witnessed. She had never seen a dead body before. There was a guilty feeling in the pit in her stomach as if she had committed the crime herself. She sat down in the basin of the bathtub and wrapped her arms around her knees as the water cascaded from the showerhead above; tears mixed with water as she cried her fear away.

Knock! Knock!

"Alija, is everything okay in there?" she heard her sister, Mickey, yell through the bathroom door.

Alija stood up and rinsed her body before stepping out of the shower. "Yeah, girl, everything's fine. I'll be out in a minute." Her voice cracked as she tried to compose her rattled nerves. She dried her body, slipped into her silk pajamas, and walked into her room. Her sister and her six-month-old daughter lay together peacefully. Alija lifted the covers and lay on the empty side of the bed as she kissed her baby girl gently on the cheek.

"You sure everything's okay?" Mickey asked as she sat up and gazed worriedly at her sister.

"Yeah, Mick, I'm good," she answered despondently as she closed her eyes.

Red filled the space between her eyelids and she quickly opened them back up.

"Oh, yeah, your baby daddy called," Mickey stated.

Alija didn't reply.

"Alija, did you hear me?" she asked.

"Yeah, I hear you. I'm just tired. Get some sleep, Mick. Thanks for watching Nahla for me."

With those words Mickey went back to sleep, and Alija tried to figure out how she would ever rest again with such a heavy burden weighing down her heart.

***

Norelle was at home, heated. She was beyond the point of sleep. She was in full-blown bitch mode and didn't care what excuse Kasheef came home with. It was going down as soon as he walked through the door. There was no stopping the neglect, jealousy, and rage she felt at that moment. She wasn't even going to try to keep her composure. World War III was in the making because the two of them were about to clash, egos and all. She heard his keys jingle in the lock, and before he could even step foot inside she asked, "See how you do me? Do you see the shit you take me through?"

He stepped into her view and when she saw all the blood on his shirt her attitude went out the window. "Oh my God! Are you hurt?" she asked frantically as she rushed to his side. The innate concern of a woman for her man kicked in and her heart instantly worried for the safety of Kasheef.

"I'm good," he stated as he gently pushed her aside.

"Kasheef, what happened tonight?" she asked, frowning at the obvious brush-off.

He sat down and put his face in his hands as he attempted to gather his thoughts. "Listen, if anybody ever asks you . . . and I'm not saying they will, but if it ever does come up . . . I was here with you all night," Kasheef instructed.

"Tell me what happened, Kasheef. Where did all of this blood come from? Oh my God, Kasheef, what is going on? You're covered in blood!" she yelled, her voice pinched in fright as she stared at Kasheef with a worried gaze, waiting for an answer.

"Norelle, stop asking all these fucking questions! Just do what I say, a'ight? You're down for your man, right?"

"Yeah, you know that," she whispered, her eyes searching his as she attempted to prove that she could be the type of woman he could trust with his life: his ride or die chick.

"Then make sure you tell anybody who comes asking that I was here all night."

"Okay," she agreed without hesitation.

Kasheef stood up and kissed her on the forehead. "Go get some sleep. We'll leave first thing tomorrow for this reunion. It looks like your little trip came right on time." She nodded and retired to their bedroom as her mind wandered into the night.

Chapter Two

"Okay. My bags are packed, all of my clients have been informed of my trip, all of my legal documents have been sent over to the courthouse, and . . ." Carmen sat at her desk and thumbed through her planner as she tried to jog her memory. "What am I forgetting, Dawn?" she asked her secretary who was standing before her with a legal pad and pen in hand.

"Did you pack your needle and thread? You know what salt water can do to a sew-in," the petite white girl replied as she looked at Carmen's hair skeptically with a playful smile on her face. She knew that her boss hated to get her weave wet and could not help but slip in a joke before she left.

"My weave is just fine, fuck you very much," Carmen replied with a smile. "I get my wig done at the best salon in New York so that's not an issue. Now what else?" Carmen and Dawn were the only young female employees at the prestigious white law firm. Most of the other women were at least twenty years older than Carmen and Dawn, so the pair naturally had more in common because they were both in their late twenties. They had worked with each other for more than five years, so they were very comfortable with one another. Carmen didn't want to be the type of boss who rode a high horse. She was pleasant and friendly. She loved to have a good time, but when she was working with a client or concentrating on a case it was all business. She took her job very seriously. Graduating top of her class at Spelman and then going on to Howard Law School made her the cream of the crop among African-American attorneys. Affirmative Action had gotten her through the door at one of the most reputable firms on the East Coast, but once she was there she found that she had to prove herself to her chauvinistic, predominantly white coworkers. They always gave her the bottom-of-the-barrel cases and she defended low profile criminals. She had to work ten times harder, and so far she had done a damned good job by never losing a case. Dawn respected her as a person, went with the flow of the ever changing work environment, and understood Carmen's desire to excel, so they vibed easily

"Let's see," Dawn said, thinking aloud. "Did you pack your condoms? God knows how long it's been since you've had some and who knows, you may get lucky. Maybe you'll find one of those sexy island men with twelve inches and a smile like Taye Diggs."

Carmen scowled while shaking her head, and replied, "You know what? You are not helping right now. Just make sure you keep everything in order here. The last thing I need is to come back from this trip and have a million and one messes to clean up."

"Yes, ma'am. Now get out of here and have fun," Dawn said, practically pushing Carmen out of her office.

Carmen grabbed her briefcase and headed out the door. She hopped into her Mercedes CLK and sped off toward the airport. She couldn't wait to unwind and have a good time with her old college sisters.

***

Things between Norelle and Kasheef were unusually awkward. An uncomfortable silence filled the space between them and they purposely avoided each other as they prepared for their trip. Norelle didn't know exactly what had gone down the night before, but she was positive that it was something serious. All of the blood had been proof that Kasheef had been involved in something illegal. The fact that Kasheef was distant and solemn let her know that he was worried about whatever had gone down. She felt like she was walking on eggshells as she moved around their home, and she silently began to question whether Kasheef could provide the type of life she wanted. She had enjoyed the fruits of his street labor by being his woman. She was known citywide, in every borough, just off of the strength that she was Kasheef's girl. Being among the hood's elite was one of the perks of being involved with a hood fella. But the negative side of the game was beginning to rear its ugly head, and she was not so sure that she could live up to the expectations of being a hustler's wife. She was expected to hold her man down at his weakest and lowest point, but knew that she would not be the one to stand tall. She did not know exactly what had gone down the night before, and it was obvious that Kasheef did not want to divulge the information to her, but she felt in her bones that whatever it was would change the direction of her life. She knew her man, and Kasheef was worried. Norelle had never seen him like this. She only hoped and prayed that he would be able to keep up the extravagant lifestyle to which she had become accustomed. The money was what made her loyal to Kasheef. If that ever disappeared, she hated to admit, there was a great possibility that she would too. It sounded cruel, but she was a practical woman; her motto was 'What's Love Got to Do With It?'

"Are you almost ready?" Kasheef asked dryly as he put on a fitted Yankees cap.

"Yeah, I'm good . . ." she replied as she grabbed her tote. She looked up at Kasheef. "Is everything okay?"

"It's nothing for you to worry about. I'll get your bags; you grab the keys to the car," he instructed.

The car ride to the airport was quiet and the silence

was deafening. After twenty minutes of driving, Norelle finally turned to Kasheef and said, "Listen, you don't have to go if you don't—"

"I'm going," he said, cutting her off. "I need to get out of the city for a couple of days anyway. Let things cool down. I'll get some sleep on the plane and be in a better mood, a'ight?" he stated.

She nodded skeptically.

"Don't worry about it. This is your weekend. Just have a good time," he finished as he kissed her forehead.

※

Kasheef and Norelle walked up to the port and were amazed at the size of the ship. Neither of them had been on a cruise before and was pleasantly surprised when they pulled up. Norelle was like a kid in a candy store, and the smile that graced her face lightened the mood for Kasheef. He had never seen her this excited. The warm Miami sun seemed to melt his cold exterior away.

They checked their bags then checked in before boarding the ship. Every single passenger on the boat was forced to attend the safety precaution meeting, so Norelle took the opportunity to look for anyone she knew. The sorority sisters weren't the only patrons on the massive ship, so Norelle had a hard time finding any of them. She figured that she would see them all at the welcome dinner that evening, so she didn't stress it too much.

"Look at this shit," Kasheef stated in amazement as they stepped into the main atrium, which allowed them to see each level of the ship.

"I know, it's crazy. I didn't expect everything to be this grand, I guess," Norelle replied.

Norelle found their ocean-view suite. The size of it reminded her of a small studio apartment in New York.

"As much bread as I broke for this room, it's kind of small," Kasheef commented as he slid the balcony door open and stepped out into the fresh air.

"It's a ship, boy, it can't be too big," Norelle laughed as she joined him. He wrapped his arms around her waist and leaned in toward her. His hard body felt good against her, and she parted her lips to meet his tongue with a passionate kiss. Her hands caressed the back of his neck, and she smiled once they pulled away from one another.

"I love you," she said.

"I know," he replied. It was a response to which she had become accustomed. She had been with him for a long time and he never told her that he loved her. She didn't need him to say it, just to know how he felt. She was secure in their relationship and was confident that he had to love her. Why else would he spend cash on her or move into her apartment and pay all of her bills? Norelle didn't want for anything, and as long as he kept her satisfied, she could live without hearing those three special words. She wasn't a child, and her fairy-tale dreams of Prince Charming had been long gone. Kasheef was as good as it was going to get when it came to a thug, and that was the only type of man that she wanted, so she accepted him as is.

"I'm tired. I think I'm going to take a shower and a nap before I get into this whole cruise thing," Norelle said. "Will you be too upset if I relax for a few hours?"

"Nah, do you, ma. I'll probably crash with you after a while. I'm going to go find a bar and have a drink or two to get my mind right. I'll come and check on you in an hour or so," he responded.

Kasheef left the room and walked through the corridors of the ship toward the main deck. There were people everywhere. Kasheef had to admit that he could get used to a lifestyle like this. Kasheef had plenty of money, but never took the time to enjoy it. He wasn't in the streets or running the streets like most hustlers. He *was* the street. He controlled every corner, every dice spot, every ho stroll . . . everything belonged to him. He was like a landlord, leasing out his properties, making niggas pay rent. If you wanted to work his blocks, you paid rent. If a ho wanted to walk on his stroll, she paid rent. He even had local businesses giving him a percentage of their profits. Needless to say, he was a very rich man. His wealth went unnoticed, though, because of his low-key demeanor. He had much love in the streets, but just like Biggie said, mo' money brought about mo' problems. He had to keep a handle on his hustling lifestyle, which was why most of his time was spent in the streets.

As the boat embarked on its three-day journey, Kasheef finally located a bar.

"Can I get a Long Island Iced Tea?" he asked the bartender.

"Can you make that two?" a feminine voice beside him asked.

He focused his attention on the young woman standing next to him. Five feet five inches with an hourglass shape and caramel skin, she was easy on the eyes. Dressed professionally in a knee-length skirt and a silk, sleeveless top, she exemplified intelligence and sophistication.

The bartender brought back their drinks, and Kasheef pulled out a wad of money to pay for both drinks. "Hey, my man, here you go," he said as he placed a twenty dollar bill on the bar top. The woman looked at him quizzically and smiled.

"You know that the drinks are included, right?" she asked.

"Nah, I didn't actually. I guess I just gave my man a nice tip," Kasheef replied.

The woman sipped her drink and said, "I guess so. Thank you for the gesture, however . . . I mean if the drinks had not been on the house."

Kasheef felt like she was trying to clown him, but he had to admit that by trying to flash his cash in front of her, he had made an ass of himself.

"I'm Carmen, by the way," she introduced herself as she held out her hand.

"Kasheef," he replied smoothly and shook it gently.

"What brings you on this trip?" she asked nosily.

"I'm running from the New York winter," he stated, not wanting to give away the fact that he was actually on the boat with his girlfriend. He knew that he wouldn't be able to do anything with the girl next to him, but he was having a good time flirting with her.

"I'm from New York too!" she exclaimed. "What part?"

"Long Island, what about you?"

"Manhattan," she said.

"Manhattan? You look like a Manhattan woman," he stated with a casual smirk.

"Excuse me?" she asked with one hand on her hip.

"Nah, ma, it's not a bad thing. You just look like you got your shit together, nah mean? Like you one of them independent sisters . . . you know, good job, more business suits than miniskirts in your closet, and no time for a man anywhere in that picture."

Her silence indicated that he was speaking the truth.

"Am I right?" he asked, already knowing the answer to the question.

"Shut up," she responded with a smile. She hated to admit to the handsome stranger that he had summed up her entire life perfectly. He had hit the nail on the head. Carmen had always been a woman who chose the career track over the social one, but because of it she was now without a man, while most women her age had partners with whom they could settle down. It was the one thing that was missing from her life. She had focused on being an independent woman for so long that now she yearned to know what it was like to be able to depend on a man. She wanted to go to sleep and wake up to the same face every day. She wished for a significant other who could welcome her home from a hard day at work. She had not realized what a great sacrifice she was making until one day she looked up and all of her single friends were married with kids.

"Maybe we can change that one day," he said.

Kasheef was charming, and Carmen blushed slightly as a flattered smile took over her face. She finished her drink and grabbed her purse. She looked him up and down, definitely enjoying what she was seeing. "Maybe," she replied. "It was nice to meet you. Hopefully I'll see you around the ship." She walked away, being sure to put a little extra switch in her hips. She turned and waved before she was out of eyesight. She would've bet her life on it that he was watching her ass, but to her surprise, he wasn't. "Maybe," she said to herself as she bit her bottom lip. She seriously entertained the thought of having a romantic rendezvous with Kasheef, but quickly talked herself out of it. *He is fine as hell though.* She shook her head, and walked away in search of her cabin.

Kasheef retreated to his room where he found Norelle curled up on the bed. He sat down on the edge and stroked her hair. "Wake up," he whispered. "You gon' sleep the whole trip away."

"I know. I need to get up anyway." She sat up and stretched in bed. "I have to get ready for the dinner."

After an hour of primping and switching outfits, Norelle stepped out of her suite looking flawless in white Ferragamo slacks with a visible crease, a white and gold Ferragamo halter, and gold Jimmy Choos. Her hair was pulled up off her face, showing off her exquisite features, the best being her two-karat diamond solitaires. Kasheef was clean in white linen slacks and a shirt. His jewelry also accentuated his fresh look.

She could tell that she looked good on Kasheef's arm because the envious looks of her sorority sisters said it all. There was nothing better than being the best-dressed and best-looking woman in a room full of other women. Her confidence was at an all-time high as she glided through the room. It was important for her to make a good impression on her old friends. She knew that after the reunion was over, she would be the topic of many conversations. If they were going to talk anyway, she was going to make sure that she gave them something to say. Her entire presence screamed new money because of the way Norelle blantantly flaunted it.

Dozens of "hey, girls" and "you look goods" floated through the room. Norelle had forgotten how fake a group of women could be. She was really only there for one person, but when she finally found her she thought she saw a hint of hater in her as well.

"Carmen!" she sang as she approached her from behind.

"Norelle!" she yelled out as she wrapped her arms around her long-lost friend. Carmen's eyes diverted to Kasheef, and a look of confusion crossed her face.

"Oh, yeah! I'm sorry, I'm being rude. Carmen, this is my boyfriend, Kasheef," Norelle said. Kasheef and Carmen shook hands as if this were their first encounter.

"Nice to meet you," Carmen scoffed.

"Nice to meet you," he replied with a smile that just earlier she was hoping to see again. Carmen rolled her eyes, thinking that all men were exactly the same. Kasheef had flirted openly with her just a few hours ago despite the fact that he had a woman. She knew he was a player. His persona had been too good to be true. He was her friend's man and therefore off limits, but the restriction only made her envious of Norelle's relationship. Kasheef was most definitely easy on the eyes. Carmen silently wondered what he may be like behind closed doors. Kasheef didn't even break a sweat. Carmen was amazed at how cool the man was under pressure.

"You look exactly the same! Oh my goodness it feels like it's been forever. How have you been, girl?" Norelle asked.

Carmen shifted her gaze from Kasheef to Norelle. "I'm doing well. I'm just working, trying to eventually make partner at my law firm. What about you? Are the two of you serious? Any kids?"

Kasheef smirked, knowing that Carmen was trying to dig up dirt and find out just how serious his relationship with Norelle was. He licked his lips and played his role of loving boyfriend as Norelle answered, "No. No kids yet, but Sheef and I are very serious. Now, you know I have never been a time clock-punching type of girl. Kasheef is a good man and he takes really good care of me."

Carmen and Norelle fell right back into their rotation and caught up on each other's lives. It had been so long since they had the time to talk, and that was a shame, especially since they lived relatively in the same area. Neither of them was surprised at how the other's life had turned out. Carmen had always been the levelheaded one, the responsible and dependable one. She had been driven in college, and her pre-law track had become a reality quickly upon matriculation. Norelle was the party girl, the free spirit, the one who rode life's waves no matter how many times she wiped out. They were so different, which was why they were such good friends. Carmen discreetly questioned Norelle about her relationship with Kasheef, but once she heard how Norelle talked about him she knew he was off limits. They told Kasheef college stories and stayed up half the night with one another.

Kasheef was glad that Norelle had found someone to occupy her time, because he had agreed to come on this trip for a reason. He had a goal to accomplish and he was going to need some privacy to do it. Norelle didn't know that his connect was located in Belize City, Belize, and that just happened to be one of the stops on their trip. He was definitely not there for laughs and giggles. He was there for bricks and money.

Chapter Three

When the cruise ship finally arrived in Belize, there was only thing on his mind: money. It was the first time he'd ever made the trip overseas to cop, so he was anxious to meet his connect face to face. The layover was only six hours, so he had to travel into the ghettos and back by the time the boat took off. Kasheef's connect arranged for him to be picked up a couple of miles from the highly publicized tourist area of the island. He caught a cab to the limo that was waiting on the side of the road for him.

"Welcome to Belize City. Mr. Solis is expecting you," the driver stated as he opened the door and Kasheef stepped inside. He saw the sandy white beaches turn into lush greenery. Paved roadways turned into undeveloped land as the driver made his way deeper and deeper into the island. Set back on top of a small mountain was a mansion unlike one he had ever seen. Its tall, plantation-style pillars and beautiful marble fountain that sat in the center of the estate went beyond his hood rich statute. He was witnessing opulence and elegance. He wanted a piece of it. He stepped out of the vehicle and made his way up toward the entrance. The doors opened on cue, and he was greeted by one of the sexiest women he'd ever seen. Her brown sugar-colored skin looked good enough to taste, and the warm smile with which she greeted him would have been enough to make him wife her. If there were ever such a thing as the perfect woman, she would have surely been it, but his fantasy of whisking her away was cut short when she introduced herself as his connect's wife.

"Hello. You must be Kasheef. My husband is expecting you," she stated without giving her name. He followed her through the opulent house and into the back of the mansion, where Osti Solis sat, birdwatching. His appearance was different than what Kasheef had expected. He was short and thin, with olive skin and dark features.

"Kasheef, it's nice to finally meet you," Osti greeted with a handshake that was firmer than expected. His body seemed weak and scrawny, but the look in his eye was cold and calculating. "I'm not what you were expecting, eh?"

"To be honest, you are not," Kasheef responded.

"The unexpected kingpin stays out of the radar. There are only two types of businessmen in this world: those who are in it for the money, and those who are in it for the recognition. The ones who are in it for the money do not like to be flashy. The unseen cannot be caught," Osti said, speaking words of wisdom that only came with years of success in the drug game.

"I agree," Kasheef agreed, while nodding his head in understanding.

"How will you get the product back to the states?"

"Money talks," Kasheef responded.

"Indeed it does," Osti stated with a laugh. He turned his back to Kasheef and looked toward the sky to peer back at his birds. "Your shipment is already in the car. Leave the money with my wife. My driver will take you back."

"You don't want to count the dough? How do you know you can trust me?"

Osti turned back around with a smirk on his face and replied, "Fear creates boundaries for men. It controls what they will and will not do. The look in my eye stops you from crossing those boundaries. That is why I finally agreed to meet you in person. So I could look you in the eyes."

Kasheef nodded and retreated to the car, where twenty kilos of heroin sat wrapped in a duffle bag. Now all he had to do was figure out how he was going to get them back on the boat.

Kasheef exited the vehicle with the duffel bag in hand. He scanned the beach suspiciously to make sure no one was watching him. He found a beach shop that sold life vests, where a teenage kid was working.

"Hey, yo', my man, you trying to make some money?" Kasheef asked.

***

Kasheef purchased twenty life vests from the beach shop, and then paid the young worker two thousand dollars to give them out for free to the passengers on his cruise ship. Kasheef boarded the ship and watched as the other passengers followed him, with complimentary life jackets in hand. As soon as they made it through customs, Kasheef stopped all twenty passengers and collected the life vests from them. He told them that Belizean products were not tested as suitable floatation devices. After telling them how unsafe the vests were and compensating them with twenty dollars each for their trouble, he was able to get the vests off of their backs with ease. They had no idea that each vest's stuffing had been removed and replaced with a kilo of heroin. It was the only way that he could have gotten the drugs on board, and although it was risky, it had worked like a charm. He quickly stuffed the life jackets back into his duffel bag and hurried to his room. He'd gotten dope past customs and was home free. He stuffed the entire bag underneath the bed and flopped down on top of it. A smile of satisfaction crossed his face. Norelle was exploring the ship with Carmen. He had gotten away with the impossible and the cruise ship was ready to make its return to the States. He couldn't have been happier.

***

"It was so good seeing you," Carmen said as she hugged Norelle affectionately. It was the final night of their cruise and they had just finished dinner. They prepared to settle in for the night. Both of them had tears in their eyes as if they'd never see one another again.

"What are we crying for?" Norelle said as she wiped her eyes and laughed. "We both live in New York. There is no excuse for us to go this long without talking again. I had fun. It's been a long time since I've had a close female friend."

"Well, here," Carmen replied, pulling out one of her business cards. "It's my card. You can call me anytime. We'll do a weekly girls' night out or something."

"Okay, girl. Have a safe trip home tomorrow."

They embraced again.

"Yeah, you be safe too. You better use that number," Carmen said as she opened the door to her cabin. "We'll get together sometime soon."

Norelle blew Carmen a quick kiss and retreated to her luxury suite where she found Kasheef passed out in the bed. She snuggled up underneath him and enjoyed the sway of the boat as it glided through the Atlantic Ocean. The setting was so romantic, the atmosphere perfect for a couple in love, but she hardly even saw her own man the entire time they were there. They were both preoccupied, she with old friends and he with his business. She admired him as he slept. He looked so peaceful, so content. She thought of the events that had occurred directly before the trip. She hoped and prayed that the drama was over, because tomorrow it would be back to the real world.

Chapter Four

It had been four days and Alija still couldn't shake what had happened. She cradled her daughter against her chest as she rocked back and forth. She looked down at her baby and smiled when Nahla cooed back at her, the child's eyes sparkling like a pool of rejuvenating innocence. Baby Nahla was the most important thing in Alija's life. She was all that her mother had to hold on to. Nahla was the only consistent and unconditional love that Alija had ever had. Her entire world revolved around her child, and her life was not her own, because she lived to make Nahla happy.

"I know, baby girl. Mommy's not going anywhere, I promise. Nobody can take me away from you," Alija said lovingly as she thought of how badly the situation at the club could've ended. It made her look at her life in a new light. Alija loved her daughter more than anything in this world and they were all that each other had. She had never felt a love as significant as the one she felt for Nahla. The emotional connection between mother and child transcended all others and she felt guilty for jeopardizing her own safety. Nahla needed a mother, a good mother, and Alija planned on becoming just that. Her club-hopping days were a thing of the past. From this day forward, she would try to better herself so that she could enjoy every moment of raising her child.

Alija placed a bottle of baby formula in a pot of boiling water, and placed the baby in her swing, then sat down at her meager kitchen table. Late notices and shut off warnings cluttered the space in front of her. It didn't matter how many times the companies sent her the letters; they weren't getting their money because she didn't have it. Alija was a product of the ghetto. A welfare baby who grew up to become a welfare mother, she had nothing. She banked on her government checks that came on the first of each month and gladly accepted them. They were the reason she did not look for a job, because she felt as if she did find a job, her monthly checks would stop coming and they would decrease her food stamps. She was better off depending on the state. She had never had a nine to five, but she always had some type of hustle. Whether it was doing hair, boosting clothes, or hustling men, it didn't matter. Anything was game as long as it helped her keep money in her pockets and food on her table.

A tear escaped from her eye as she thought about what she had been through in the past couple of days. It had put a fear in her heart that she had never known, and she knew that she had to do something. It was her responsibility to provide for her family and keep her daughter safe. She needed some money so that she could move her daughter out of the hood and start a new life for them both.

Nahla's hungry cries erupted throughout the room, signaling Alija to check on the bottle. She removed it from the boiling water, tested the temperature on the inside of her wrist, and then scooped up her daughter. "What am I going to do, baby girl? We all we got, mama." Her daughter greedily sucked the bottle. Alija smiled, and she carried her daughter in her arms as she went to check the mailbox. She was waiting for some paperwork from the state. She had a scheme brewing and she was anxious because it would put some extra money in her pockets. She had convinced her caseworker to give her a $1200 car voucher. The car that she currently owned wasn't registered in her name, so it wasn't hard for her to get the naïve white woman to issue her a car credit. She already had one of her girls lined up, ready to purchase the voucher for $800 cash. It was a quick way to make some easy money. She never even worried about the repercussions of her actions. It was her way of working the system, but she was tired of depending on the system altogether. She was looking for her way out; she just hadn't found it yet.

She carried the mail back into her apartment and frowned when she saw something addressed to Mickie from the US Department of Justice. "Oh, shit," she mumbled as she lay Nahla down on the couch for a nap. She hoped that her sister hadn't gotten caught up trying to defraud the welfare offices. She knew that if Mickie got caught she wasn't going down alone. She'd be the first one coming to Alija, talking about "Girl, they got us." Alija quickly opened the letter and a sigh of relief escaped her once she saw what it was. It was only a request for Mickie to appear for jury duty selection at the end of the month. She put the letter in her sister's room and then went back to sorting through her bills, trying to figure out which ones she could afford to pay this month.

* * *

"Ooh, right there, Sheef," Norelle moaned as her man's muscular body rested atop her own, moving in a slow rhythm. His body was so toned and dark. The way that he was making love to her made her back arch and her toes curl. "I love you," she whispered as she rolled onto her stomach, changing positions so that he could enter her from behind, while she played with her feminine pearl. Kasheef admired Norelle's perfect body before filling the space between her legs. He rocked in and out of her, kissing the nape of her neck at the same time. He felt her body quiver as she reached bliss, and with a few deep strokes he joined her in satisfaction. Norelle immediately turned on her side and fell asleep while Kasheef arose to take a shower. After washing his muscular body briefly, he went into the living room and turned on the TV. He couldn't believe what he saw.

"This is Sunshine Miller reporting live for NY1 News. This is the scene where a vicious murder was committed only a week ago. Mizan Simmons's body was recovered yesterday by two fishermen who found the deceased floating face down in the Hudson River. After tracking his whereabouts with friends and family, the police were led to this night club. It is in fact the last place Mizan was seen alive. The following tape that we are about to air has just been released by the New York Police Department."

Kasheef's jaw hit the floor when he saw a videotape of the inside of his club. It showed him and Mizan inside the office, with Alija in the background, peeking through the door. Kasheef's heart felt as if it would beat out of his chest as he watched himself shoot Mizan on the local news station. It then showed him run out of the room after Alija, and later showed three of Kasheef's goons come to clean up the murder scene. Luckily for Kasheef his face was not recognizable, but to his dismay Alija was easy to identify and he instantly regretted letting her walk out of the club alive. She was the only person who could identify him as the shooter, and he was sure that the police would be looking for her. That only meant one thing: he had to get to her first.

***

Alija dropped the remote control as she listened to the news broadcast.

"The extent of this crime is so drastic that the police have released this private footage in order to find citizens who may have any information regarding this offense. The police are asking for help in solving this brutal murder. The NYPD have confirmed that the victim was a suspected drug dealer, so it is a very good possibility that this is a drug-related murder. If you know anything that can help in their investigation, or if you recognize anyone in this video, please contact the police at (212) 965-0800. Funeral services will commence tomorrow night for Mr. Simmons. The public is welcome to attend. Back to you, Bob."

"Oh my God," she stated. The ringing of her phone caused her to jump.

"Hello?" she answered, her voice barely audible.

"What in the fuck did you get yourself into? I just saw your face all on the news. Is that what happened the night you came in crying?" Mickie asked. She was talking a mile a minute.

"I don't know, Mick . . . ." Alija responded nervously. Tears swelled in her eyes and a huge lump formed in her throat. "I don't know. I was there and it all happened so fast. I just panicked. I saw him get killed."

"And now the whole world knows it," Mickie stated.

"What am I gon' do?" Alija asked.

"You gon' lay low, that's what. Just chill out and don't say nothing to nobody. You've still got to live in the hood. You ain't got the money to get out, so don't let them pigs talk you into snitching. You've got my little niece to think about. I'll be home in a couple of hours. We'll talk more then," Mickie said.

"Okay," Alija answered before hanging up the phone. She went into her bedroom, grabbed her baby from her crib, and lay in bed. Her skin crawled as she thought about how her life had just taken a turn for the worse. For some reason she was afraid to turn out the lights. She stared at Nahla and knew that she was in danger. "I've got to get us out of here, baby girl . . . soon."

***

"Yo', as soon as these lights go out, we're in there. Hit everything moving. Sheef said he'd rather be safe than sorry, so shorty got to go," Stick instructed as smoke from his blunt escaped from his full lips. He sat outside of the apartment building with two goons behind him. They were there to do a job; to exterminate a problem. They were all working on behalf of Kasheef and knew the importance of what they were about to do, because they were the same boys who had cleaned up the murder scene at the club. Their asses were on the line as well, so they had to do the job and do it right. Stick popped the magazine into his 9 mm as he leaned his seat back, and then watched the building.

"Let's just do this. I ain't sitting here all night, yo'," one of the dudes complained.

"Sit ya' ass down, fam. When the lights go out, we go in . . . and not a minute before," Stick replied.

***

Alija couldn't keep her eyes open any longer. She slowly arose from her bed and flicked the lights off as she prepared herself for a restless sleep. Nahla began to whimper beside her and she looked over and stroked her chubby cheeks. "What's wrong, mama? Huh? You want your binky?" she asked lightly. Alija arose from her bed and tucked Nahla in snugly so that she couldn't roll off, then went to retrieve her daughter's pacifier. She had to move quickly because she knew she would never get any sleep if Nahla got cranky. She made her way down the hallway where her daughter's diaper bag was sitting by the front door. "Shit!" she mumbled as she stubbed her toe on her coffee table while making her way through the dark. She bent down to grab the bag, but froze when she heard voices outside her front door.

"Kill everybody in this mu'fucka. We're not leaving any witnesses."

Alija's breath caught in her throat as she put the strap of the diaper bag across her body. She peeked out the peephole and saw three men standing outside with guns in hand. She sprinted back to her room, knocking into furniture on the way. She heard the lock to her front door click and the door open and close, but she didn't look back. She ran for her life until she reached her room. She knew her house better than her assailants, and was able to make it to her daughter before they figured out which way she'd run. She closed and locked her bedroom door, then grabbed her daughter off the bed, trying her best not to make her cry.

Nahla began to whimper and Alija rocked her as she looked back and forth around the room, trying to figure out where she could run.

"Shh! It's okay," she whispered as silent tears graced her face. *What the fuck am I gon' do?* she asked herself. All of her windows were barred so that wasn't an option. She remembered the crawl space above her bed. It was only a small attic-like space and she wasn't even sure if she would fit inside, but she had to try. She jumped on top of her bed and reached up to remove the ceiling tile. She hurriedly place Nahla inside first before she hopped up herself, the diaper bag still hanging from her body. Just as she slid the ceiling tile back in place, her bedroom door came crashing down.

"Bitch, where are you?" one of the men yelled as he snatched open her closet door. He created so much noise that she felt Nahla stir.

God, please don't let her wake up. Please, she prayed as she put her hand over her baby's ear and brought her closer to her chest.

"Kill all that noise," Stick instructed. He looked toward the window. "The bitch got bars on her windows so she's in this mu'fucka somewhere. Find her."

Alija slowly rocked back and forth as she heard the men tear up her house, overturning furniture and all in their attempt to find her hiding place. Alija was terrified and she didn't know what was going to happen. She feared for the life of her daughter and she only hoped that the intruders would give up their pursuit. She heard their footsteps travel into the living room, and her heart froze when she heard a knock at her front door.

Knock! Knock! Knock!

She heard her intruders panic.

"Oh, shit! It's the police, fam," one of them whispered.

Knock! Knock! Knock!

"Open up! NYPD!"

It was the first time in her entire life that she was happy to have the police at her house. She stayed in her position, quietly contemplating her next move.

"Sit down and act normal . . . Hurry up and turn this furniture back over and stash them pistols," she heard one of the intruders whisper harshly.

Stick opened up the door and greeted the police, "Hello, officers. What can I do for you?"

"We had some complaints from some neighbors about a disturbance," one of the officers replied as he stood firmly in the doorway with his hand positioned on his gun holster.

"We probably did get a little loud, officer. You know how it is when you get together with the fellas. I apologize," Stick answered, laying it on thick.

The police officer looked around at the group of men suspiciously. "Is there anyone else in the house?"

Stick could've shit himself when he heard the female voice behind him say, "No, sir, it's just me and my daughter's father and a couple of his friends." She walked out of the room with her daughter held snugly in her arms. Her eyes darted wild-

ly around the room as she tried to remember the faces of the
men who had come to do her harm.

Stick shifted uncomfortably in his stance as he stared a
hole through Alija. The officer immediately recognized her face.

"Ma'am can you come with us please?" the officer asked.
"You are wanted for questioning in relation to a murder that
happened about a week ago."

"A murder? My girl don't know nothing 'bout a murder,
officer," Stick answered as his forehead began to sweat.

"I can come with you," Alija said eagerly, while silently
thanking God for showing her a way out.

The officer nodded and responded, "You may want to
leave the child with her father, miss."

"My daughter goes where I go," she said harshly. "Now
I'm ready to make a statement."

She walked out of the apartment with Stick grilling her
as she walked past. He was lucky she didn't turn him and his
friends in. He smirked once he realized the game that the girl
had just run on him and his crew. He respected her gangsta,
though, because she didn't snitch him out. He just hoped that
she lived by the same code when it came to the murder.

"What was that?" one of the goons asked.

"I don't know, fam, but let's get the fuck outta here before our luck runs out."

Chapter Five

That was so stupid. I should've turned them in. They are only going to come back for me, she thought regretfully to herself. *They're probably watching my crib right now . . . I have to warn Mick.*

She tapped her leg against the floor rapidly, while holding Nahla in her arms. The police had contained her in a questioning room for over an hour, and she just wanted to get this over with. She wasn't a snitch, but she planned on telling what she knew in order to protect her daughter. The door finally opened and a tall, lean man stepped inside the room. He was dressed casually in slacks and a blazer, his badge hanging on display from his belt.

"Hello, Alija, I'm Detective Neilson," he said. "Do you need anything? Are you hungry?" His voice was friendly, but Alija was no dummy. She had been born and raised to hate the police so she knew he was playing the good cop role, she just wondered where the bad cop was hiding. "Can you tell me what you know about the night of March twenty-first? What happened at Club Blaze that night?"

Alija was quiet and her attention was on her child. She was hesitant to look at the detective, and she sighed deeply.

"We know you were there, Ms. Bell," he said, using her last name.

"His name is Kasheef, he owns the club," Alija said in a low tone.

"Is he my shooter?" the detective asked eagerly as he leaned into the steel table.

Alija nodded.

"And you will testify to that?"

"If that is what it takes to protect my daughter, then yes. Now I need to call my sister."

***

Kasheef held Norelle in his arms as an uncanny feeling suddenly swept over him. He sat straight up in bed and looked around his room. It was too calm inside of his bedroom. It was as if the entire world had come to a standstill. He didn't hear the usual voices of the corner boys who were out trying to make a day's pay, or the sound of neighbors coming in from a late night out; even the hum of the refrigerator had ceased. Everything was silent, too silent, and the hair on the back of his neck stood straight up. He shook his head and told himself that it was just paranoia.

"What's wrong, babe?" she asked as her brow furrowed with concern.

"Nothing, it's just too quiet in this mu'fucka," Kasheef replied, trying to shake the caution that his sympathetic nervous system was sending out. "Something just doesn't feel right."

Norelle pulled back the covers and revealed her naked, perfectly sculpted figure. "I know something that feels right. Come back to bed," she enticed as she opened and closed her legs seductively.

Kasheef crawled on top of her. Their tongues intertwined in a passionate kiss, but they were interrupted by the hinges being knocked off of their front door.

Norelle and Kasheef jumped out of bed, but before they could do anything their bedroom was swarmed with fully suited SWAT agents who held automatic weapons pointed their way.

"Get on the ground!"

"Get on the ground now!"

"Kasheef?" Norelle screamed as she was handcuffed and put face down on the floor.

Detective Nielson approached Kasheef and slapped the silver bracelets around his wrists. "Kasheef Williams, you have the right to remain silent—"

"I want a lawyer," he said calmly and cockily as he cooperated fully with the police. He turned up his nose smugly and looked down at Norelle, who was also being read her rights.

"Norelle!" Kasheef called out to her.

With her hair wild and her face stained with tears, she looked at him. He shook his head from side to side and she already knew what the code meant. He was telling her to keep her mouth closed. Silence was the key when dealing with the police. It was something that the couple had discussed before, but talking about it and having it actually happen were two completely different things. Norelle could feel the panic setting in as she closed her eyes.

Detective Nielson pushed Kasheef toward another officer and yelled, "Get him out of here!"

Before the officer could respond, another cop came into the room with a black duffel bag. "We've hit the jackpot," he announced as he unzipped the bag. The heroin that Kasheef had copped from Belize was packed neatly inside.

Kasheef instantly began smacking himself for keeping the product inside his crib, but he knew that it was a charge he could beat because the apartment was not in his name. The detective finished reading Kasheef his rights as he was escorted out of the building.

***

"I don't know anything!" Norelle screamed for the millionth time as Detective Nielson asked her the same questions over and over again. "Why are you doing this to me?" she asked. She was distraught. Her hair was a mess and the knots in her stomach gave her a queasy feeling. It felt as if her dinner would come up at any moment. The police detective was quickly backing her into a corner. She was trying to stay strong and not reveal what she knew, but with every threat Nielson threw her way, he chipped off a piece of her allegiance to Kasheef, and she began to think of saving herself.

"You did this to yourself, sweetheart. Dating a drug dealer must make you hot shit, huh?" he grilled. He leaned in so close to her that she could smell the scent of old tobacco on his breath, and she had a front-row seat to his crusty, crooked teeth.

Norelle was silent as she put her face in her hands and shook her head from side to side. She just wanted to get out of there. All she wanted to do was go home and forget that any of this had ever happened.

"Where were you the night of March 21, 2008?"

"I was at home," she answered.

"And where is home?" the detective asked.

Norelle frowned and rolled her eyes. "Where did you arrest me at?" she shot back sarcastically. Her voice was full of irritation as she smacked her lips and sat back in her chair.

"So that is *your* apartment?" Nielson asked again, purposely repeating himself to make sure that he established her residency.

"Yes! How many times do I have to tell you? Yes, that is where I live," she replied. She had no idea that she had already said too much. The police were merely giving her enough rope to hang herself. With every word that she said, she tied the noose tighter and tighter around her neck.

"Where was Kasheef on the same night?"

"I already told you he was home with me," she answered.

"All night?"

"Yes," she replied.

"What time did you go to sleep?" he asked.

Norelle didn't know how she was supposed to answer that question. She was growing frustrated and confused. "I don't know. I can't remember. Don't I get a phone call or something? I know my rights; you cannot just hold me here like this. I want to make a call."

***

Carmen looked over at her nightstand when she heard the irritating shrill from the ringing of her phone. "It's four o'clock in the morning. Who is this?" she said in exasperation. She picked up the phone. "Hello?" A sigh escaped her lips as she waited for a response.

"C . . . Carmen?"

Carmen sat straight up in her bed when she heard the distraught voice. "This is Carmen. Who is this?" she asked.

"It's me. I . . . It's Norelle."

"What's wrong? Are you okay?" Carmen asked.

"I'm in jail. I've been arrested and I need a lawyer. They're trying to get me to say things about Kasheef. I didn't know who else to call," she stammered.

Carmen threw the bedspread from her legs and hopped out of bed. She ran to her closet and pulled out a grey Donna Karan business skirt and silk blouse. "No, it's okay. I'm on my way. Don't say anything to anyone else until I get there, okay?"

"Okay," Norelle said before the line went dead.

"What in the hell has this girl gotten herself into?" Carmen pondered aloud as she slipped into her clothes. She unwrapped her hair and combed it down around her face, and slipped her feet into black, three-inch designer pumps. Grabbing her keys and her briefcase all in one swift movement she ran out the door.

***

"You know you're going to go to prison, right?" the detective taunted. "Twenty kilos of raw heroin inside your apartment. Whoo! That's a lot of time. You'll never get out, and a pretty little piece like you will drive the butch broads crazy."

"Those drugs aren't mine!" she protested.

"So they belong to Kasheef?" Detective Nielson asked, feeling like the girl across from him was getting ready to crack at any moment.

As soon as Norelle opened her mouth to speak, the door opened forcefully.

"This interview is over," Carmen stated. "Let's go, Norelle." She helped her friend out of her chair and then nodded toward Nielson. "Detective."

"Counselor," he replied with a nod. He could've protested and held Norelle longer, but she wasn't the type of fish he was looking to fry, so he let her walk for the time being. He wished he had even a minute longer with her because he had a feeling that she was getting ready to talk. "I'll be in touch," he promised.

Carmen stopped dead in her tracks, turned on her expensive heel and stared directly in the detective's eyes. "If you need to speak with my client about anything, be sure you call me first," she said in a professional but threatening way. She wrapped an arm around Norelle and ushered her out of the precinct.

"Carmen, I don't know what to say. Thank you," Norelle said once they were outside.

"Don't worry about it. Go home, get some sleep, and we'll meet for breakfast tomorrow morning to discuss everything. By then I'll have a lot more information about what they may be trying to charge you with."

"Can you get him out?" Norelle asked despondently.

"Not tonight, but that's what we'll work on tomorrow. Go get some rest, girl. You're going to need it," Carmen suggested. The two women embraced and then went their separate ways. Norelle had the weight of the world on her shoulders and Carmen a huge smile on her face. She needed a major case like this. More importantly, she needed to win a case like this. She was trying to make partner at her law firm, and a case like this could make or break her career. She just hoped she was ready.

***

"What am I going to do?" Alija asked. "They could've killed me and Nahla."

"But they didn't, sis, that's what's important. Thinking about what could've happened will drive you crazy," Mickie comforted her as she held her baby niece and paced the floor of the motel room Alija had checked into. "You can't go back to the apartment, especially now that you're snitching."

"Thanks, Mick! That helps," Alija responded sarcastically. "What other choice did I have, huh?"

"I'm just saying, Alija. You don't even have any cash to relocate. You can't snitch on somebody like Kasheef and then go back to the hood thinking shit gon' be gulley. His people gon' be gunning for you just off of GP," Mickie said.

"Well, either way I'm losing. He sent them dudes up in my crib before I said one word to anybody. I had no intention of going to the police," Alija objected.

"It's done now. You've already started telling. Now you need to think about how you gon' live after all this is over. This ain't a game."

"No, it's definitely not that," she responded as she looked at her daughter. "This is my life, Mick . . . It's her life."

Chapter Six

Carmen walked into her office to find her boss sitting in her chair. She was surprised, and greeted him hesitantly as she sashayed toward her desk with a copy of the morning *New York Times* tucked beneath her arm.

"Good morning, Richard," she said as she sat her Dooney & Bourke alligator-skinned briefcase near her feet.

"Carmen . . . I hear you've taken on a major case," he stated.

"What case might that be?" she asked, unsure of what he was speaking of. Richard stood up from her desk and stepped out of her way as he motioned for her to take a seat. He reached for the remote control for the small plasma television in her office. Flicking on the screen, he turned to the local news station, catching the middle of the broadcast.

"Kasheef Williams's arrest occurred early this morning. A police representative states that they are charging Mr. Williams with second degree murder. By obtaining a noted defense attorney by the name of Carmen Rose, it is definitely not an open-and-shut conviction for the prosecution. Ms. Rose is a junior associate at Barnes & Baker Legal Firm in Manhattan and has not lost a case in the five years she's been practicing law . . . ."

Her boss turned off the TV before the broadcast could finish playing, and looked her in the eye. "Are you sure you want to take on a case of this magnitude?"

Carmen fidgeted in her seat. It was true that she had never lost a case, but her record was jaded because she had never defended a crime more serious than aggravated assault. Murders, rapes, and drug-related offenses were usually handled by the senior partners . . . more specifically, the white male senior partners. She was up for evaluation in six months and she desperately hoped to be considered for the open position of senior partner. With her record she had a good chance, but her competition was sure to argue about the ease of the cases she'd previously tried. She needed to take a chance on a major case. Kasheef's case had just happened to fall into her lap. "Yes, Richard, I'm sure."

"Okay, then . . . I can say this off the record. If you bring this win in for the firm, I can almost guarantee that the board of trustees will elect you as the new senior partner. You have full access to all resources, paralegals, or research teams you may need."

A huge smile crossed Carmen's face as her boss turned to leave. Before he exited fully, he faced her once more. "But if you lose, Carmen, it will set your career back five years. Everything you've accomplished will be overshadowed by this loss."

"I guess I have to win then," she stated confidently. Dawn walked into the office with an incredulous look plastered on her face.

"Is what they're saying on the news true? Are you really getting ready to defend Kasheef Williams?" Dawn asked.

"I guess so," Carmen replied with a slick smile. "If I can pull this off I'm taking you straight to the top floor with me, Ms. Executive Assistant." She got up from her seat and glided past her secretary. "I'm going to meet with Kasheef's girlfriend to discuss her involvement in his activities. After that, I'm going downtown to let Kasheef know I'll be taking his case. I still haven't spoken to him."

Carmen made her way to Starbucks on Lexington Avenue, and ordered two caramel macchiatos as she waited for Norelle to show up. Ten minutes passed before Carmen saw her friend come through the doors. She waved her over and instantly felt bad when she saw Norelle's swollen, red eyes. She could tell that her girl hadn't gotten much sleep.

"Thanks for coming," Norelle said while pulling out a chair and graciously accepting the macchiato. She shifted in her seat nervously and then looked up at Carmen. "I can't go to jail, Carm. I'll do whatever I have to do to get out of this situation."

"What exactly is the situation?" Carmen asked. "If I'm going to represent you, I'm going to need to know everything. You can't keep anything from me."

"Kasheef wasn't home that night, Carmen. He didn't come home until, like, four in the morning. There was blood on his shirt," Norelle admitted.

"Do you think Kasheef committed this murder?" Carmen asked as she took notes on a legal pad.

"Yeah, I do." Norelle was ashamed to say it. She had bragged and flaunted Kasheef in front of Carmen, lying about what Kasheef did for a living to make herself look better. Now the truth had come out and she was forced to admit the truth. She did not want to tell Carmen about what had happened that night. Kasheef had given her specific instructions to be his alibi, but she was so afraid that she was just looking for a way out of her predicament. She didn't care who she had to throw under the bus in order to do it.

"And the drugs?" Carmen asked.

"I didn't even know they were in the house," Norelle replied incredulously.

Carmen reached over the table and grabbed her friend's hand. "I need to go speak with Kasheef. Try to get some rest, okay?"

Norelle nodded.

"I'll call you later," Carmen said before walking away.

**

"Williams, let's go!" an officer yelled as he came and removed Kasheef from the bull pen, placing him securely in cuffs.

Kasheef stood without protest and was taken to a small interview room. He stepped inside and noticed Carmen sitting in front of him.

"Norelle sent me," Carmen explained. She turned toward the officer. "Can you remove the cuffs?"

The officer unlocked the handcuffs and left the room. Kasheef massaged his wrists as he sat down in front of Carmen. "Thank you for coming," he stated. The crease in his forehead and the way that his brow dipped low revealed his stress. "What do they have on me?"

"Kasheef, I'm not going to lie to you. I don't like to paint a fairy-tale portrayal of any case just to sugarcoat what is happening. I would rather be upfront and honest with you so that there will be no surprises. I want you to know what to expect of my services."

"I respect that," he replied. "Just keep it real with me. What am I facing here?"

"This does not look good," Carmen stated frankly.

"I know . . . I know. My back is in a corner right now. You've got to get me out," Kasheef said with pleading eyes.

"They have a witness. This entire case relies solely on her testimony. I've seen the tape from the club that night. Your face isn't recognizable, which works in our favor. I will play on that fact as much as I possibly can. She's the only person who can place you at the crime scene," Carmen said. She hesitated before continuing. "I need to know everything, Kasheef. Don't try to hide anything from me. I'm a lawyer. If you want me to do my job effectively I have to know what went on that night. I have to know the complete truth, not just what you interpret it to be. Did you do it?"

Kasheef leaned across the table until he was only inches away from Carmen's face. "I'll tell you what I'm not gon' do: this time they're trying to stick me with. Get me off." His voice was low as he spoke, but it did not stop the authority from being present in his words. Carmen understood perfectly. She knew men like Kasheef. At one time in her life she had been attracted to men just like him. He was a boss and he was used to being in charge. He never asked for anything from anybody. He demanded respect and instilled fear in the hearts of many. He was not the type of man you could tell no, and she understood this. She nodded, knowing that he would never admit his guilt. He didn't trust her enough to incriminate himself and she could understand why. His life was on the line. Her gut told her that he was guilty, but her mind told her that it didn't matter. She was going to do her job to the best of her ability. Whether Kasheef committed the murder was irrelevant. She would do all that it took to sway a jury into finding him innocent.

"Okay," she said as she closed her briefcase and stood to leave. "You're being arraigned later on this afternoon and we'll enter a plea of not guilty. I'll try to get the judge to set bail. See you in court."

***

Alija watched from her car as Mizan's friends and family slowly scattered from his grave site. She didn't know why she was there, but she felt compelled to go pay her respects to him. She had seen everything that had gone down the night he was murdered. She wanted to get out. She wanted to shed tears over his grave, but something kept her rooted in her car. She knew that she was not welcome. She knew the full story. She saw Mizan try to rob Kasheef, and then in the blink of an eye the situation turned in Kasheef's favor, and Mizan was the one who ended up dead. The tears that tainted her cheeks were those of sadness, regret, and fear. Kasheef knew that she had witnessed his actions, yet he let her go. Now she was scared, running for her life because she was getting ready to testify.

She looked in the back at Nahla, who was sound asleep in her car seat. She closed her eyes as she thought of all the things that her daughter would miss out on because of the tragedy that their lives had become. *You can fix this,* she told herself. *All you have to do is testify against Kasheef. After the trial all of this will be over. You can just pack up and leave.* She knew that she didn't have much, but she was willing to go as far as a full tank of gas would take her just to get out of New York. Just as she pulled away from the curb, her cell phone rang.

"Hello?" she answered.

"They really fucked up our apartment," Mickie said.

"I know, tell me about it. Do you think it's smart for you to be there? What if they come back?"

Mickie scoffed and replied, "They're not looking for me. They want you and after all the attention they drew the first time, they won't be trying to come back here. I'll be fine."

"Okay," Alija replied skeptically. "Oh, yeah, I forgot to tell you that the state sent you some papers. I set 'em on your bed. Something about jury duty."

"Yeah, okay . . . good looking out. I'ma get myself thrown out of that selection so fucking quick. What I look like, sitting on somebody's jury all damn day," Mickie replied.

"I know, right?" Alija replied. "I'll call you later. I've got to go get my mind right."

"Say no more . . . I'll come through later on with the la after I figure out what's up on this jury bullshit," Mickie said before hanging up the phone.

***

"On the state charge of second degree murder, how does the defendant plead?" the judge asked.

"Not guilty," Kasheef said.

The judge looked toward the prosecution's desk. "Is the state prepared to proceed to trial?"

"Yes, we are, Your Honor," District Attorney Nancy Swartz replied.

"Okay, then, jury selection will begin immediately. If both counselors agree, there is a jury pool taking place today at 3:00 P.M. This jury pool was originally for another case, but this case takes precedence. Jury selection can begin today. Now let's proceed to the matter of bail," the judge stated.

The DA stood and said, "The state is asking for remand."

Carmen immediately stood and interjected. "Your Honor, that is completely unreasonable. My client has no prior record and does not propose a flight risk. He insists that he is innocent, and on his behalf I must ask for a personal recognizance!"

"On a murder trial!" the DA said with mocking laughter in her voice.

Carmen knew that she was grasping at straws by asking for Kasheef to be released on nothing but his word, but it was all part of her plan. If she low-balled, when the state countered her offer it would be around the right ballpark. Otherwise the DA would try to stick her client with a high bail, and she was going to fight tooth and nail to prevent that from happening. "Your Honor the state has nothing but circumstantial evidence against Mr. Williams. Their entire case relies solely on one woman's testimony."

Kasheef smirked to himself as he watched Carmen in action. She was passionate about what she did and he was glad that he had her on his team. He was confident in her skill.

"She's an eyewitness!" the district attorney shouted.

The judge banged his gavel and sighed. "Ladies, there has to be a medium that we can come to." He paused and thought for a moment. "Bail is set at $200,000 cash or bond."

Carmen smiled as Kasheef was handcuffed.

He nodded her way and said, "Send Norelle down with that bail money. I want to be out of here like yesterday."

***

"This is some bullshit. They got me up in here for some damn jury selection," Mickie complained.

"It's not that bad," the lady beside her commented. "They pay you ten dollars an hour just to be here."

Mickie rolled her eyes, but perked up a little bit as she thought about getting paid for nothing. A young black woman and an older white woman entered the room. They were assigned numbers and then pulled into a small room one by one, where the defense and prosecuting attorneys asked a series of questions to determine the jury. When Mickie's turn rolled around she walked into the room and took a seat. She wore Seven jeans under an ivory New York & Company pea coat.

"Please have a seat. I'm District Attorney Nancy Swartz," the white woman said.

"Mickie," she replied as she sat down.

"And I'm defense attorney Carmen Rose," Carmen said. "You are here to be considered as a juror on a very high profile case. A man by the name of Kasheef Williams has been accused of murder. Does this case sound familiar to you?"

Whaaat? Ain't this about a bitch? I'm sitting here getting considered for Kasheef's case. "No, that doesn't sound familiar," Mickie lied. She didn't know why, but she felt compelled to get on this case now that she knew all that it entailed.

"Mickie, have you ever been arrested or involved in any illegal activities?" the DA asked.

Mickie thought of all the times she'd defrauded the welfare offices. "No, I've never done anything illegal."

"How do you think drugs have affected your community?" Carmen asked, trying to gauge if the young woman had any personal vendettas against drug dealers.

"I guess I don't really think about it," Mickie said. She tried to sound neutral on the situations so that she could appease both the prosecution and the defense. She felt like she was at a job interview as her palms began to sweat.

"When choosing between two sides, what do you base your decisions on?" the DA inquired as she stared intensely at Mickie through wire-framed glasses.

"On the facts that I've been given. I try to keep things as real as possible," Mickie said.

The DA looked at Carmen, who then said, "I have no more questions. Thank you, Mickie, we'll be in touch."

She smiled as she walked through the decadent halls of the historical courthouse. She couldn't wait to tell Alija what had just taken place. They were in a position to turn the tables.

***

Alija and Mickie sat outside of the motel room smoking la as Mickie described what had happened earlier that day. Alija thought that it was ironic that Mickie had gotten requested to sit on the same jury to a case where she was the prosecution's star witness.

"So what, have they picked you yet? Are you on the jury?" Alija asked as she took the dutch from her sister's fingertips and brought it to her lips, inhaling deeply. She looked back at the open motel door to make sure her daughter was still asleep.

"Nah, not yet. I'm just a consideration, but I played both sides of the field when they were asking me all the questions. If things go like I think they're going to go, I'll be getting something in the mail requesting me to come back."

"This is some crazy shit, Mick. How we both twisted up in this web?" Alija asked as she laughed out loud.

Mickie began to laugh too as she draped one arm around her sister. "What the fuck is so funny?"

Alija really started cracking up once she heard Mickie's question. "What you laughing for if you don't know why I'm laughing?"

"Bitch, I don't know," Mickie replied as she wiped the tears of laughter from her eyes. "This some good shit."

Alija smiled and blew out more smoke. "Yeah, it is . . . cuz I don't even know why I'm laughing. Ain't nothing funny about my life right now."

"I've been thinking," Mickie said. "What if I get elected to this jury? You're the only witness in Kasheef's case. If you really look at it, we're holding his freedom in our hands."

Alija passed the dutch back to Mickie and looked at her with hazy eyes. "What, you trying to blackmail him?"

"Not blackmail, I'm talking extortion. If you're testifying you're gonna need some getaway money," Mickie said.

"I'm willing to bet he'll pay anything to beat this charge," Alija commented.

Nahla began to cry and Alija stood, dusting off her clothes before she went inside. Mickie followed close behind as she watched her sister pick Nahla up.

"What do you think?" Mickie asked.

"I don't know, Mick. We could be opening up a whole new can of worms . . . creating new bullshit, and stepping into more problems," Alija said.

"You forgetting about what you saw? What you've been through?" Mickie said. "You probably haven't even thought about how this murder has changed you and Nahla's life."

"That's all I've been thinking about, Mick! That's why

I have to be smart. Nahla needs me. I'm all she has," Alija protested.

"And you need some money to get out of here once this is all over," Mickie urged.

Alija nodded. "Just let me think about it."

Mickie hugged her sister and said, "I love you, girl. Everything is going to be okay, but you seriously need to get with this and jump on this opportunity. It's the only way you're ever going to feel comfortable again without watching over your shoulders. Make shit happen, sis . . . don't let it happen to you."

"Yeah, a'ight . . . I told you I'll think about. Just give me a little bit of time."

Chapter Seven

The next morning, Norelle popped open Kasheef's safe. She knew that he had both Swiss and Cayman accounts, so the money inside the steel safe was just the tip of the iceberg. Since Kasheef's arrest she'd been conflicted in her loyalties. A part of her wanted to stand by Kasheef. He was her man and Norelle did care about him. In fact, she loved him, but she was quickly discovering that her feelings were only worth the dollar amount he spent on her. Kasheef had bought her affection by showering her with lavish gifts. When he was on top, Kasheef was the most handsome man in the world to her. He was her everything and she was willing to do anything to keep him happy so that she could keep her spot secure as his woman. She loved money, and he had a lot of it that he was willing to share with her, so in turn she loved him. But he was in jail now and her relationship was on rocky ground. Her fear of being dragged down with him caused her to consider her options.

She looked at the neatly stacked bundles of hundred dollar bills. The safe was filled from top to bottom, and she estimated that there was at least three hundred grand in the safe alone. If Kasheef kept this much money in the house, she could only imagine what he had in his accounts overseas. She pulled out $25,000 and put it in her Berkin bag before heading out to meet Carmen. She arrived at the Manhattan law firm thirty minutes later, and was greeted warmly by Carmen as she took a seat in one of the plush leather chairs in her office. She had to admit how impressed she was. Her girl was doing well for herself. She pulled out the money and placed it on top of Carmen's desk.

"Here's the first payment for Kasheef's case. I know that's only a quarter of it. I can bring back more if you want," Norelle said as she sat back and folded her legs.

"No, this is fine for now. I'll be sure to keep my time on record so that we can settle the balance later," Carmen said. "I have good news for you."

"What's that?"

"Kasheef can come home," Carmen stated.

Norelle smiled slightly, unsure if she was really ready for him to get out of jail. With Kasheef locked up, Norelle had full access to his funds. There was enough money in that safe for her to relocate and start over, without the drama of Kasheef. With that much money she didn't need to find a new man to take care of her. She would be able to provide for herself. "Oh, okay. Well, when will he be getting out?" she asked.

Carmen removed the money from her desk and put it in a manila envelope. She then put the envelope in a small safe behind her desk. "As soon as you can get $200,000 to post his bond. He can be out as soon as today," Carmen said.

"I didn't think the state allowed you to come out on bail in a murder case," Norelle said with a frown on her face.

"They don't. I'm just that good," Carmen bragged as she winked playfully at her girl. "As long as Kasheef stays out of trouble and keeps his court dates while we're going through the initial stages of the trial, he should be able to stay out of jail. The fact that the state's evidence is weak helped him out a lot."

"Oh," was all that Norelle could manage to say.

"I have a press conference scheduled today. I'll bring this case to the public from the defense's perspective and paint him to be wrongly accused. It's always good to have the community behind him," Carmen stated.

"What about the drugs?" Norelle asked.

"That's a completely different charge and will be prosecuted under federal jurisdiction. The federal courts haven't even brought an indictment against Kasheef for that yet, so we'll just focus on getting him off for the murder right now," Carmen said. She noticed Norelle's disposition and frowned. "Smile; your man's coming home. All you've got to do is go down there and get him." Carmen stood from her seat and looked at her lady Movado watch. "I don't mean to cut this meeting short, but I've got to get out of here. The press conference starts in twenty minutes. Call me if you need me."

Norelle got up and walked out of the office. Her head was all over the place. She thought about the money that was in Kasheef's safe. He had more than enough money to post bail, but she had no intention of getting him out. *If he goes to jail, that'll leave me with nothing but time and opportunity to spend his money.* Murder carried a twenty-five years-to-life sentence. She'd have nothing to worry about if he was convicted.

Norelle thought back over the last two years during which they had been together. She tried to manufacture times that he'd done her wrong or cheated on her. She thumbed through her mental Rolodex searching for just one memory that could justify her actions. A time he'd hit her or belittled her. All she needed was one instance to give her a reason to take his money and leave him rotting in jail, but she couldn't come up with anything. Kasheef had treated her well and upgraded her tremendously when they started dating. She had not a need or want in this world because of his generosity. A twinge of guilt swept over her as she thought about all the times he'd made her smile. She knew she was wrong, but she didn't care. Money made her world go 'round, and now that she had an opportunity to backstab Kasheef, she was going to take it. *It's all in the game*, she thought as she made her way home.

***

"My name is Carmen Rose, and as you know I am representing Kasheef Williams. Mr. Williams is innocent and my team of legal consultants are doing all that we can to exonerate him of these false allegations. Keep in mind that Kasheef Williams is an upstanding figure within his community. He has donated countless hours to shelters in Long Island during the holiday seasons, and even financed a youth basketball team in his neighborhood. If you listen to the rumors that are circulating regarding Mr. Williams's involvement in illegal activities, you will only be contributing to the corruption of these charges. Now I will take any questions that you may have." Carmen was in rare form as she stood on the courthouse steps and smiled for the cameras from all of the major news stations. She answered questions from the press professionally and handled herself like the star she was. She was bringing major coverage to Kasheef's case and knew that it would help them in the courtroom. The jurors were sure to have seen the coverage, and she hoped that it would help paint a pleasurable picture of her client. As the press conference came to an end, she walked toward the black Lincoln Town Car that was waiting curbside for her. She turned toward the camera one last time and said, "I hope that all of you outstanding individuals will use the media as a way to spread a positive light on Mr. Williams's situation. We don't want the public to sensationalize the lies and ignore the truth. Justice is what we are seeking." She watched the media eat up her words like steak and potatoes, and then disappeared into the car.

One of her paralegals sat beside her and looked back at the mass crowd of reporters. "Wow, you definitely got their attention."

"That was the point," Carmen replied as she melted into the leather seats and closed her eyes. "The prosecution is sure to respond. It will be cat and mouse, tit for tat, until opening statements. Let the games begin."

***

The first thing Norelle did when she got home was open the safe. She needed to know exactly how much money she was working with. She pulled out each bundle and admired each stack that was perfectly wrapped in rubber bands. She lay all of the money out on her bed and began to count. The smell of the money was like a narcotic to her senses; her fingertips tingled at the touch of each hundred dollar bill. It was a diligent task, counting that much money, but it was one she welcomed. There was so much money in front of her that she lost count several times, but she never complained. She eagerly started from the beginning, making sure not to miss one bill. It was what she called a good problem. It took her hours, and when she was done the grand total was $325,000. She was ecstatic. She brought a handful of bills up to her nose and inhaled deeply, smelling her newfound riches. She threw the money into the air and fell back onto the bed in sheer glee. "Aghh!" she screamed at the top of her lungs to release some of her excitement. She lay down in the bed, a feeling of triumph rushing over her body. She knew what men meant now when they said money made their dicks hard. In between her legs was soaking wet. She slid her finger inside her panties. Her phone rang, interrupting her from pleasing herself.

"Hello!" she said once she'd snatched up the phone.

"I have a collect call from Rikers Island Correctional Facility for Norelle Gibson. Will you accept the call?"

"Yeah, I guess," she answered.

Kasheef's voice filled the receiver. "Yo', Norelle, you talked to Carmen?"

"I left her office earlier today," she said in an innocent tone.

"Why you ain't post my bail this morning? These mu'fuckas done shipped me from city lockup to Rikers Island all because you didn't handle that," Kasheef said, obviously irritated.

"I'm sorry, Sheef. Carmen said that there were some papers she still needed to file, but that I could come bail you out first thing in the morning," she said convincingly. "You know I wouldn't do you like that, babe. I'm over here sick without you. I'm playing with my pussy right now." Her voice purred and she massaged herself gently as she closed her eyes and pictured Kasheef in her bed. She had to admit that's one thing he was good for.

"Word?" he asked, on the verge of an erection. He could picture her spread eagle on their satin sheets, and the image was tantalizing.

"Yeah, baby. I can't wait for you to come home," she whined.

"Then come and get your man," he said.

"Don't worry, boo, you'll be home first thing tomorrow," she assured him.

"Yeah, a'ight," he replied. "Keep that hot for me. I got to get off of this phone, but I'll be waiting on you tomorrow, Norelle."

"I got you, Sheef," she said and then hung up the phone. "Yeah, right, nigga!" she yelled to herself as she continued to please herself. Her body tensed as she brought herself to an orgasm. When she was done, she rolled over on the bed full of money, pulled her covers around her body, and fell into the most luxurious sleep she'd ever had.

***

Alija watched the woman on the television as she portrayed Kasheef as a model citizen. Alija was disgusted, and frowned as she thought of how he had ordered his cronies to run in her apartment. She knew that the young boys were on a ghetto execution mission and she thanked God that the police had shown up when they did. A knock at her motel door startled her and she pulled back the curtains in the room to see outside. Detective Nielson stood with his hands in his pockets, and she opened the door to greet him.

"Hello, Alija," he said as he glanced nosily inside the room.

"No one is here but me and my baby," she said as she motioned for him to come in. "What can I do for you, detective?"

Detective Nielson looked around the downtrodden room and asked, "When's the last time you got some fresh air?" When she didn't respond, he continued. "Why don't you let me take you to grab a bite to eat? There are some things that I want to go over with you regarding the trial."

Alija nodded and replied, "Okay. Just give me a minute or two to get Nahla ready."

"I'll be waiting in the car."

Alija slipped her daughter into a knit sweater, tiny jeans, and winter booties. It was freezing outside and she wanted to make sure that Nahla was dressed warmly. She put her in the car seat, threw a blanket on top of it, and headed out to the detective's car. After securing Nahla in the back she hopped up front.

Detective Nielson took her to a nice Italian restaurant on the lower east side. Dinner was awkward and silence filled the air as the two ate together.

"How do you feel about testifying?" he asked her.

"Like a snitch," she replied bluntly.

"You are not doing anything wrong," Nielson replied. "People like Kasheef Williams deserve to be locked up."

Alija shook her head. "You just don't get it. Where I come from you don't snitch. You learn that from the very beginning. When you're little, nobody likes a tattletale; when you're older, nobody tolerates a snitch. I'm putting everything on the line to testify in this case, but right now I feel like I'm damned if I do; damned if I don't."

"This no snitching rule is what is keeping the inner cities from prospering. It is something that has been drilled into your heads, but it is a bunch of bullshit. It stops the good guys from winning," Nielson stated angrily.

"I guess it's just a difference of opinion," Alija said stubbornly. She did not expect the detective to understand. She did not doubt that the hood had trained her and programmed her a certain way, but she was sure that the state had trained the detective as well. They were from two different worlds; like oil and water, the two did not mix.

"The prosecution will want to work with you before the trial. The DA needs to prepare you for the defense's rebuttal," Nielson said.

"That's fine," she said in a low tone. She looked up at the television that hung in the corner of the restaurant. Ironically, the exact same case that she and the detective were discussing was being reported on the screen. Alija stared at a picture of Kasheef on the screen. She stared into the eyes of the man she was expected to help put away. She picked up her baby, who had begun to cry, and she looked at the detective.

"Damned if I do, damned if I don't."

***

Kasheef was growing tired of sitting in prison. Another day had passed with no word from Norelle. He knew that Carmen had handled everything on her end, because he had called her to make sure. *I'm trying to give this bitch the benefit of the doubt.*

He looked around the empty cell. He recalled his last conversation with Norelle. She hadn't showed him any shade. The words that she had spoken to him had seemed sincere, but he couldn't get rid of the nagging feeling in his stomach that something was wrong. During the entire two years that he had been with Norelle he had trusted her wholeheartedly. She had never betrayed his trust. He even tested her on numerous occasions, by leaving money around or by simply leaving his cell phone sitting out in plain view. Her honest heart never allowed her to lift a dime that didn't belong to her, and her confidence always made her bypass his cell without checking it to see who was calling her man. Kasheef almost felt guilty for assuming the worst in his girl, but her actions were causing his guilt to fade and his suspicions to grow. What he didn't know was that Norelle was only with him because of what he did for her. Now that he was locked up, he didn't serve his purpose. She was a money hungry bitch who had slipped through his gold-digger radar, and now she had her claws in his back.

His thoughts driving him to his breaking point, he couldn't contain himself any longer. He had to find out why he was still sitting behind the thick brick wall. He walked out of his cell and stood in line for the phone. His mind was playing games with him, causing him to become enraged. He tried to control his temper; he didn't want his rage to get him into any complications with the other prisoners. He was well aware of his own strength and ruthlessness, so if any of the inmates ever stepped to him he would surely gain another murder charge. He had to remain cool and distance himself until he got out. He desperately needed to get out. Twenty minutes later the line to the phone finally decreased and he picked up the receiver and dialed the operator.

"You'd like to make a collect call?" the operator asked.

"Yes," he replied.

"To what telephone number and to whom?"

"516-845-9812, to Norelle Gibson," he said.

"Hold please."

The line went silent for thirty seconds. The operator came back on the line and said, "The collect call was not accepted."

"What?" he yelled into the phone. "Nah, that ain't right. Maybe you dialed the wrong numbers. I'd like to place the call again."

The operator repeated the same procedure, placing another collect call. Kasheef waited impatiently until the operator finally said, "I'm sorry, sir, the collect call was not accepted."

Kasheef slammed down the phone. "I see how this bitch trying to play me," he said to himself as he returned to his cell. He was more than livid. He was ready to kill Norelle, and it was then that he knew she was not to be trusted.

***

"I have a collect call from Rikers Island Correctional Facility for Norelle Gibson. Will you accept the call?"

"Hell no!" Norelle said as she hung up the phone for a second time. She grabbed three fat stacks of hundred dollar bills and put them into her purse as she headed out. "I think it's time I got myself a new whip," she said as she hopped into her '04 Cadillac Escalade truck and drove to the dealership.

By the end of the day, she'd copped an '08 Lexus convertible coupe. She had also linked up with a realtor who was helping her shop for a brand new condominium. She already had the home furnished in her head. She had put deposits down on furniture all over the city, so that once she found a place, all she had to do was have her furniture delivered.

It was taking her no time to blow through Kasheef's

money. By the end of the day she had spent an easy seventy grand. She had never had that type of money in her possession in her life, and now that she did, she didn't know what to do with it. She was on a shopping spree, and for a woman as materialistic as Norelle, having that much paper to burn was like heaven. She couldn't remember a time when she'd been happier. Clothes, shoes, and cosmetics gave her confidence. Cars and jewelry made her feel important. There was nothing better to her than rolling through the streets, having everyone notice her. Money distinguished her. It put her on an entirely different level than other women. *It's bum bitches at the bottom and Norelle at the top*, she thought arrogantly as she made her way back to her apartment. She was enjoying her newfound wealth, and once she spent the first dollar, all thoughts of it ever belonging to Kasheef were erased from her mind.

Norelle struggled with the many bags that she carried as she tried to find her keys to unlock her apartment door. Her phone began to ring on the inside and her frustration caused her to drop her bags. "Damn it!" she screamed. She decided to leave the bags where they were for the time being, and sprinted to the cordless telephone.

"Hello?" she answered as she looked back at her front door to make sure her bags were still in the hallway. An old woman passing by stopped and eyed the bags curiously.

"I have a collect call from . . ."

Norelle stopped listening when the old woman reached into one of the bags. "Are these bags yours?" the elderly woman asked.

"Yes!" Norelle yelled as she shooed the woman away.

"Okay, I'll connect your call," she heard the operator say once she'd refocused on the telephone.

"Wait, no! I didn't accept . . ." she tried to decline the call, but was interrupted by Kasheef's voice.

"Why you ain't taking my calls, Norelle?"

"Baby, I am. What are you talking about? You haven't called me since the other day," she said, trying to play off her deception.

"I called your ass two times earlier and both times you didn't take the calls," he said. "Bitch, you trying to leave me in here on stuck? Where's my fucking bail money, Norelle?"

"Kasheef, what are you talking about?" she asked as she tried her hardest to muster fake tears. "Nobody called me earlier! I would've accepted the charges, you know that. The operator must have dialed the wrong number. And I don't have the money to bail you out. The police came in here with a warrant and they took all of the money out of the safe!" She sobbed uncontrollably and put on a genius performance, one that might've gotten her an Academy Award if she had chosen to be an actress instead of a gold-digger. "I'm out here trying to hustle up bail money for you and you're calling me on this bullshit."

"When did they run in the house, Norelle?" Kasheef asked.

"Yesterday. I've been waiting for you to call so I could tell you. That's how I know the operator got the number wrong earlier because I would have accepted the call. I'm out here all by myself scared and worried every day about you," she cried, adding a loud sniffle for dramatic effect, while rolling her eyes in the mirror.

"A'ight, ma," he said with a sigh. "Stop crying."

"I can't believe you would think I'd turn my back on you," she whispered.

"I don't think that, Norelle. These walls are just fucking with my head. Look, yo', I've got to get off this phone. I'll call you tomorrow, a'ight?" he asked.

"Okay," she responded and hung up. She looked in her

vanity mirror and quickly wiped away the fake tears. "Sucker-ass nigga."

***

Mickie tore open the letter from the Department of Justice and jumped up and down when she saw the words You Have Been Summoned to Jury Duty printed in big bold letters. She knew that this could work to her advantage if she wanted it to. She picked up the phone and called Alija.

"Hello?" Alija answered.

"You'll never guess what I'm holding in my hands right now," Mickie said without even saying hello or stating her name.

"What, Mick?" Alija asked, automatically recognizing her voice.

"The key to your future, baby sis," Mickie said matter-of-factly.

"If it ain't a million dollars then it can't open any doors for me," Alija joked.

"I don't know if it's worth a million, but it can damn sure get us some money!" Mickie replied. She couldn't contain the excitement in her voice.

"Girl, what are you talking about?" Alija finally asked.

"I've been summoned," Mickie said.

Alija got quiet as she weighed her options. She really didn't have anything to lose. She was in a lose-lose situation so she figured that she may as well try to get some money to take care of Nahla. She didn't want to pull Mickie into it, however.

"I'll do it. I'll blackmail him under one condition," Alija said.

"What is it? Anything." Mickie replied.

"You have to let me handle it. I don't want you involved, Mick. If something does happen to me, I need to know that Nahla has someone in this world who will look after her. All I need you to do is sit on that jury and have my back when I need it, okay?"

"Okay, Alija."

"And we probably need to distance ourselves for a while. We can't be seen together at all. No talking to each other. We have to act like we don't even know one another until after this trial is over. I need you to be on that jury, Mick. You are my ace in the hole in case something goes bad. If the jury is going to come back with a verdict that I don't like, I'm gonna need you on there to sway their asses in my direction," Alija explained. "When I get the money from Kasheef, you know I'm going to look out for you."

"I already know, sis. I just wish that there was more that I could do," Mickie complained.

"You're doing enough already, Mick. Just trust me. Don't contact me. We have different last names so no one will ever figure out that we are related as long as we are careful. My name isn't on your lease at the apartment so we should be good. Just keep everything quiet. I'll be in touch with you, okay?"

"Okay. I love you, girl, and be careful."

"I will," Alija answered, then hung up the phone. Alija was scared because she knew that she was playing with fire. She kept telling herself that she had nothing to lose and everything to gain, but she knew that was untrue. She had her daughter to lose and the one thing that she didn't want to leave behind in this world was a motherless child. She hoped that God would see her through this. She had never been the religious type, but she knew that she could not do this alone and He was the only one she could think of to call on.

She grabbed her daughter in her arms, humbly got down on her knees, and silently prayed, *Dear God, I know you don't hear from me often, but I'm coming to you today. I'm burdened. My heart aches in a way that I have never felt before. My life is out of my hands. I feel like I'm losing everything and I need your help. For me to even be on my knees right now means that I need you. Nahla needs you. Please give me the strength to make it through this trial. I'm just trying to provide a better life for my daughter, the best way that I know how. Give me the courage to go through with this. Please. Amen.*

Chapter Eight

Beep! Beep! Beep!

Carmen sighed as she removed her sleek Fendi reading glasses and threw them onto her desk in frustration. She was trying to find a loophole in Kasheef's case, but she was having a hard time concentrating. Every time she got focused, another distraction caused her to slip up. If it wasn't the ringing of her telephone, then it was a knock at her door. This time it was the beeping of her intercom system.

"Yes, Dawn?" she asked dryly as she held the intercom button down.

"I have an Alija Bell here to see you," Dawn announced.

"Alija Bell?" Carmen asked as she tried to recall the name. Her eyes widened in surprise as she finally remembered where she had heard it before. "Alija Bell as in the star witness to the Williams's case?"

"I believe so. She says she has some information that you may be interested in hearing," Dawn stated.

"Okay, send her in," Carmen said as she closed Kasheef's case file and stood up to greet her guest. Curiosity was killing her. She could not imagine what the star witness in the biggest case of her life could possibly want, but she could not wait to find out. She walked around the desk when the girl walked in and she immediately recognized her from the tape that she'd watched of Kasheef's crime. "I take it you are the woman the prosecution has found to solidify their case?"

"That would be me," Alija responded as she extended her hand toward Carmen. Carmen looked skeptically at her hand and then shook it firmly.

"I'm not sure what it is I can do for you," Carmen admitted. "Technically, you're not supposed to be here."

"It's not about what you can do for me, but what I can do for you . . . or more like Kasheef."

Carmen folded her arms and leaned against the front of her desk. "What could you possibly do for my client, Ms. Bell?"

"I could change my testimony," Alija responded frankly.

Carmen tried to hide her shock behind her sophisticated demeanor, but Alija had just thrown her a curveball. Alija was the only person who was standing in her way of a victory and now here she was in the flesh, offering to switch sides.

"We both know that I can identify Kasheef. He was there and he killed Mizan, and unfortunately, I'm the only one who saw it. I didn't ask to be put in this situation. I'm not in the business of ruining lives; I'm just trying to live mine."

"Why are you offering to do this now? What changed your mind?" Carmen asked suspiciously.

"I was never going to snitch from the beginning. Kasheef started this when he sent his little workers to my house and make sure you tell him that. I'm just trying to come up with the best solution for both of us," Alija stated.

"I don't know anything about Kasheef sending anyone to your home, Ms. Bell, but I'll deliver the message. What if I told you I didn't need you to change your testimony in order to get Kasheef off?" Carmen stated confidently.

Alija laughed before replying, "You're not that good. Let's be real. We both know that if I testify against Kasheef there is no way he will walk."

Carmen hated to admit it, but no matter how well she

performed her job she felt like there was a great possibility that she would blow this case. The defense was at a disadvantage and an offer like the one she was being given didn't come every day. She needed this win. Her career depended on it. "How much is it going to cost him for your cooperation?"

"$200,000," Alija said.

"As you know, a matter like this is a sticky situation. I'm putting a lot on the line by even considering this. Just this conversation is putting my job in jeopardy. Don't misunderstand that what you are doing is illegal and if you are caught I will deny any participation in this arrangement," Carmen stated seriously in a low tone so that no one outside of her office door could pick up on the conversation.

"I understand," Alija said.

Carmen sighed deeply. "Let me discuss some things with my client and I'll get back with you. Is there a number where I can reach you?"

Alija shook her head. "No. As you said, this is serious business, so let's not leave a paper trail. I'm staying at a Motel 6 out in Long Island, room nine. If you need to speak with me, come there and come alone. My offer is only good for forty-eight hours."

"I'll be in touch," Carmen stated as she finished writing down the information that she was just given. She put the pen down and opened her office door. Alija began to walk out. "Oh yeah, and Ms. Bell?"

Alija stopped dead in her tracks and turned around.

"Don't come to my office again. If you need to talk, call me and I'll come to you." With that Carmen closed her office door. She couldn't believe the turn of events that had just taken place. A sly smirk crossed her face as she thought of how her new office on the top floor was going to look.

Carmen walked out of her office and stopped at Dawn's desk. "Can you forward all calls to my voice mail? I need to make the trip to Rikers today and it'll probably be an all-day trip."

"Sure, is there anything you need for me to do?" Dawn asked.

"Yes, actually there is, but I need you to be discreet. Find out as much information as you can on Ms. Alija Bell," Carmen said curiously.

"Sure. What case file would you like me to put the information into?" Dawn asked.

"Just put the information in my right desk drawer. It's not for a case. I just need to know more," Carmen replied before walking out of the door.

***

Kasheef was relieved when his name was called. He knew that it had to be a visit from Carmen. It was the only time that the COs pulled inmates out of their cells without questions. He had been driving himself mad thinking about Norelle. He knew in his heart that the excuses she had given him were lies, but his pride hoped that he was wrong about her. He would be humiliated if his suspicions were confirmed and she turned out to be a snake.

He got up and walked slowly through the tier toward the front of the prison, until he came to a crossroads. To his left was the exit from the facility, to his right was the interview room where Carmen awaited him. He looked left for a second and hoped that he would one day be able to take that route.

He walked in and, as usual, Carmen was stunning in her designer suit. Today she wore glasses, which left an image in his head of a sexual fantasy he'd once had of a school teacher. He chuckled to himself and shook the image from his mind. He'd definitely been in jail for too long.

"Why are you still here, Kasheef? Why haven't you posted bail?" Carmen asked in confusion as worry lines creased her forehead.

"That's what I'm trying to figure out," he replied. "Let me ask you something, Carmen, and I need you to be honest with me."

"Go ahead."

"Have the police gotten any new warrants to search my home?" he asked. He stared her directly in her pupils so that he could try to detect a lie if one slipped from her pretty lips.

"No, why would you ask that?" she inquired.

"So the police haven't confiscated any new evidence?" he asked.

"No, they haven't. Honestly, Kasheef, the police have more than enough evidence to make their case," Carmen said.

That lying-ass bitch. I would have given her anything but she had to be greedy. She's trying to go against the grain and play me like I'm stupid . . . grimy-ass bitch.

"Kasheef, I have to talk to you about something. Something private that can't leave this room, you understand?"

"Yeah, speak your mind, Carmen," he said.

"Alija Bell stopped into my office today . . ."

"What?" he asked in exasperation.

Carmen looked around and leaned into the table. She lowered her voice. "She told me to tell you that she would've never come forward if you hadn't sent your hit squad to her house."

Kasheef gritted his teeth as he listened to his lawyer speak.

"She says that she's willing to change her testimony on the witness stand and say that you are not the man she saw shoot Mizan Simmons," Carmen said.

"Does that mean I'll walk?" he asked.

"She is the key to the prosecution's case. Without her, the murder charge won't have much to stand on. If she keeps up her end of the bargain, I believe we'll win. The judge may even throw out the case against you."

"What is our end of the bargain?" he asked.

"She wants $200,000 and we only have forty-eight hours to respond," Carmen said.

"Make it happen," Kasheef said. He stood up. "Thanks for everything, Carmen."

"Don't thank me yet. This is far from over, but things are looking better for us," she said with a smile.

Kasheef returned her smile and then walked out of the room. By the time he got back to his cell it was recreation time. He immediately got in line for the phone. After a short wait, he placed a call to his man.

"Yo', Stick!" he said once he was connected.

"Oh, shit, I know this ain't who I think it is. What's good, fam? How you holding up in there?" Stick asked.

"I'm good, baby. Listen, I need you to come through with that bail money for ya' boy. Its twenty stacks, but you know I'm good for it. I'm just having a little trouble catching up with my chick, nah mean?' Kasheef stated.

"No doubt, fam, I'll be there first thing tomorrow. I saw your girl pushing a new whip the other day. She showing shade now that you caught the case?" Stick asked, already knowing the answer to his question. He wasn't one to categorize all females into the same category, but bitches like Norelle never stuck around when the heat blazed. When things were good, champagne was flowing, and money was long, they were happy, but as soon as it was time for their loyalty to be tested they ran dry. He had never cared for Norelle and could see through her gold-digging tactics, but out of respect for Kasheef he kept his mouth closed and showed her love. Now her true colors were bleeding through her cheap visage, and Stick felt bad for his mans for falling into her trap. Many a nigga had been left broke behind some woman who had stuck them for their paper, and gotten ghost when they were supposedly doing a bid with their man.

"Yeah, the shady bitch thinks she slick, but I got it under control," Kasheef said calmly. "Just make sure you come through, a'ight?"

"Yeah, I got you."

"One," Kasheef said and then ended the phone call.

Kasheef grinned to himself. He couldn't wait to hit the streets. He knew that he would have to lay low so he wouldn't be able to get at Norelle the way that he wanted to, but he was definitely going to see her. He had something else in mind for her, however, something that she would never see coming. He also needed to settle a score with Alija Bell. He would pay her a visit too, just to be sure about what the terms of their agreement really were.

***

Carmen placed a call to Norelle to inform her of the latest developments of the case.

"Norelle, I have some good news for you," Carmen stated as soon as her friend picked up her cell.

"What? You sound excited. What is it?" Norelle asked eagerly.

"I think your man is going to win his case. At first I was worried because the evidence against him was so concrete," Carmen stated.

"Well, what the hell changed?" Norelle asked, coming off more harshly then she intended to. She needed Kasheef to be found guilty. She had already fucked him over. It was too late for her to turn back. She had lied to him and had already begun spending his money. She knew that her disloyalty was not something that Kasheef would be willing to forgive, and although she had never seen his violent side, she did not doubt his gangster. She knew exactly what he was capable of and did not underestimate his ruthlessness. His hood status in New Yitty had been what had attracted her to him, besides the money, in the first place. Money. Power. Respect. To Lil' Kim it's the key to life; to Norelle it was the key to her heart and the treasure between her thighs. But those were qualities that Kasheef could not hold on to behind bars, and because of his downfall, Norelle had changed her locks. At one point, Kasheef had it all and she had wanted a piece of the pie, but she knew that she had bitten the hand that fed her. Now she had to find a way to keep his ass locked up. *Why this bitch got to be so damn good at her job?*

"The only witness in the case offered to recant her testimony," Carmen stated.

"She did what?" Norelle asked. "How did this come about?"

"The girl wants money, what else?" Carmen scoffed. "I talked it over with Kasheef and he thinks it's a good idea, so we are going to go for it."

"Are you sure this is a good idea, Carm?" Norelle said, trying to plant seeds of doubt and uncertainty in her girl's mind. "I mean, I love Kasheef and I want him out of jail more than anyone, but isn't this illegal? Couldn't he get in more trouble for this? Better yet, what about your law career? You could be disbarred!"

Carmen had already weighed all of her options. She knew exactly what was at stake, yet she was willing to take the risk. A career without advancement was equivalent to having no career at all, so she was about to take her chances. With a victory from this case, she would sky rocket to the top. Everything was about to blow up for her. Her career would be at an all-time high. Salary. Ego. Benefits. The sky would be the limit. She would be her own boss.

"I've thought about all of that already, Norelle," Carmen said. "Honestly, this is Kasheef's only shot at freedom. I know what I'm doing. You leave the law up to me and I'll make sure that your man comes home for good."

That's what I'm afraid of, Norelle cursed silently. "Well, where is Sheef now?" she asked with a sigh.

"He's still locked up in Rikers," Carmen responded. She frowned and continued. "Why haven't you bonded him out yet, Norelle? He doesn't look good. I mean, he's not physically ill or hurt, but when I look at him I can see the burden on his face. It seems like he is carrying the world on his shoulders. He really needs to be home, you know?"

"Yeah, I know, Carm. I'm trying my best to come up with the money. Twenty stacks does not come easy these days. I should have the rest of the money by the end of the week. I planned on getting him out then," she lied as she rolled her eyes. "But, listen, how far away are you from the city? We can do lunch or something."

"I'm not close at all. I just left Rikers and I have some things I need to look into when I get back. I'm going to have to take a rain check."

Norelle busted a U-turn and headed toward Carmen's office. "Okay, well, I'll call you later." She disconnected the call and threw her cell phone in her lap out of frustration. "Ughh!" she yelled as she hit the steering wheel repeatedly.

Fifteen minutes later, Norelle found herself pulling up in front of Carmen's workplace. She walked into her office as if she belonged, and found that no one was sitting at the secretary's desk in front of Carmen's office. She let herself in and walked over to Carmen's desk. Her hands shook as she ruffled through the many papers and manila file folders that were scattered on top of the desk. She tried to hurry so that she could get in and out undetected.

"Where is it? Where is it?" she mumbled impatiently. She finally located Kasheef's case folder. She thumbed through it, quickly reading some of the details of the case. She located the name of the witness in the case. *Alija Bell.* She went over a brief bio on the girl. *Now all I have to do is find you.* She continued to rummage through the papers until she found a piece of paper with Alija's address on it. It was for a motel and she figured it had to be what she was looking for. *I think I might pay this bitch Alija a visit myself,* she thought as she recopied the address on a piece of paper.

She was just about to leave the office when she heard voices outside of the door. She saw the doorknob turn. *Oh, shit.* She ducked underneath the desk and pulled her knees close to her body so that she would fit. Her heartbeat was erratic and her nerves were shot as she tried not to breathe too loudly.

"I'd like to view the case file on Mr. Williams's case," she heard a male voice say.

"Sure, no problem. I'm sure Ms. Rose left it somewhere on her desk," a feminine voice replied and sat down in the chair. Norelle flinched as she tried to avoid contact with the woman's legs, which were inches from touching her. She scooted as far into the small space as she could and closed her eyes, praying that they wouldn't find her.

Norelle's eyes shot open in dismay when a pungent smell wafted up her nostrils. She almost threw up in her mouth when she noticed that the smell was coming from between the legs of the seated woman. *This is what I get for trying to snoop,* she thought disgustedly as she took in as little air as possible. She felt like she was choking on rotten fish. *God, please let her find this damn file before I die underneath this mu'fucka.*

"Oh, here it is!" the woman announced, and then the legs and deathly smell disappeared. Norelle waited until she heard the door open and close before she burst from underneath the desk, gasping for air. She was sure to return everything to its original condition then she snuck out of the office undetected, with a frown on her face.

***

"Mommy is gonna get us out of here, baby girl," Alija said as she fed Nahla a bottle and watched TV. She was watching the local news to make sure that she was on point with what was going on in Kasheef's case. There had been coverage on it at least twice a day, and she felt like she needed to be involved in every aspect. She was attempting to swindle a very dangerous man, and she wanted to make sure she was aware of the circumstances surrounding the situation.

She was nervous, and had been waiting for a visit from Kasheef's legal defense. When day turned to night she feared that maybe she had asked for too much money. *What if they don't pay up?* There was no guarantee that Kasheef would even be interested in taking her up on her offer. *Maybe I shouldn't have given his lawyer my address. What if she gives my info to him? He can just send some of his goons here to finish me off.*

She noticed that her daughter's bottle was empty. She put the baby over her shoulder and gently patted her back while walking around the room nervously. A car door slammed and she walked to the window to see who was outside. She didn't recognize the woman, so she walked away while still attempting to burp her child.

Knock! Knock!

Alija frowned. She answered the door and stared into the eyes of a woman she didn't recognize.

"Can I help you?" she asked.

"Are you Alija Bell?" the woman asked.

"Who are you?" Alija replied as she looked the woman up and down, her arched eyebrows raised in defense.

"My name is Norelle. I'm Kasheef's girlfriend. Can I come in?" she asked as she shivered from the winter's cold.

"No," Alija replied bluntly and began to close the door.

Norelle stopped the door from closing with her hand and shouted, "I want to pay you to testify against Kasheef!"

Alija's chin dropped to her chest and her eyes grew wide in surprise. "What?" she asked incredulously. "Did you say against him?"

"Can I come in? Please," Norelle asked again, this time almost pleading to gain entrance. She needed Alija to send Kasheef away to prison.

Alija moved to the side and allowed Norelle to step into the room. Norelle tried not to turn her nose up at the horrible accommodations.

"You can have a seat," Alija offered.

I'm not sitting my ass on that filthy chair. As a matter of fact, let me hurry up and get out of here. "No, I won't be long. I heard about the offer that you made to Kasheef's lawyer this morning. You see, Carmen Rose is my best friend from college, which is why she chose to defend him. The reason I'm here is because I need you to testify."

Alija put her hands on her hips and interjected. "Look, I've already told your man's lawyer what I'm willing to do—"

"I want you to testify *against* Kasheef!" Norelle blurted out, interrupting Alija.

"What?" Alija asked in confusion. She had thought she had heard the girl wrong the first time, but she wasn't deaf or dumb.

"Yeah you heard me right. I would like to pay you to tell the jury what you saw that night," Norelle said.

Alija peered at Norelle. She didn't know if she could trust her. It was obvious that she had no type of loyalty toward Kasheef. *Her ass was probably living nice while he was out and doing good. Now he's locked up and she's trying to keep him in,* Alija thought in disbelief.

"Why would you want me to send Kasheef to prison?" Alija asked suspiciously. Growing up in the hood she could peep a fake bitch when she saw one, and the girl in front of her was as phony as a Chinatown Coach bag. She did not have room to make any mistakes, and she had to be extremely careful in the game she was trying to play.

"Look, it's not in my best interest for Kasheef to beat this case. I never expected him to come home. After he was arrested I ran off with some of his money and stopped accepting his calls from prison. He's sitting in there waiting for me to bail him out, but he'll be waiting for a while, if you know what I mean," Norelle replied frankly.

Alija turned up her face as if Norelle stunk. *This bitch is dirty. It's fucked up how she's trying to play him.* Alija was reluctant to deal with Norelle. She figured if she had turned on her own man, then she definitely couldn't be trusted.

"I know what you're thinking," Norelle stated. "But I feel like no one can judge me but God. I know it seems bad, but I'm just trying to look out for myself. I can't think about Kasheef. Shit, he did not think about me! He chose to be in the streets and I know just as well as you that he killed that man. That's on him. I refuse to suffer behind his bullshit. I can't do that time with him. I'm not the one to be stressed and making monthly trips to Rikers. That shit is for ugly women who can't replace their sponsors. Me, I have them lined up around the corner, so there is no point for me to stay with Kasheef."

Alija thought of what Norelle had just said, and although she didn't like the girl, she had no right to judge her. *I guess it doesn't matter who I get the money from as long as I get it.*

"I'm willing to give you $75,000 if you tell the truth on the stand. All you have to do is tell what you saw and Kasheef will go away for at least twenty years," Norelle stated.

Alija looked at the clock on the nightstand. It was ten o'clock and Carmen still hadn't gotten back to her. She figured Norelle's $75,000 offer would be a good backup plan in case her other deal fell through.

"Let me think about it for a couple of days and I'll let you know," Alija replied.

Norelle wrote down her cell phone number on a piece of paper and handed it to Alija. "Call me when you decide," she said, and then walked out of the room.

Alija looked at the number and rolled her eyes as she tossed it onto the dresser. She wasn't comfortable with Norelle knowing where to find her, but she didn't have a lot of money to relocate to a different motel, and going home was definitely out of the question. She picked up the phone and dialed the office.

"Hi, this is room nine. I'm having some issues with the heater. It's blowing out cold air. Can I get transferred to the room next door?" she asked. She'd rather be safe than sorry. She had to stay one step ahead of the game.

Chapter Nine

"Williams, let's go! You made bail," the corrections officer yelled as he opened up Kasheef's cell. Kasheef couldn't jump up fast enough. He knew that he would be able to count on Stick. He was his protégé, and Kasheef was confident that Stick's allegiance to him would not fade just because he was locked up. He checked out of the prison, not even stopping to get his belongings because he didn't want to stay inside the musty walls a moment longer than he had to.

"Sheef!" Stick shouted as he extended his hand and embraced him quickly in one swift motion.

"Good looking out, fam," Kasheef replied. "You know I got you. As soon as we hit New Yitty, I'ma hit you with some cash and bless you with a little something for coming through for your boy."

Kasheef and Stick made the trip back from Rikers as music pumped loudly from Stick's custom subwoofers. Both men nodded their heads simultaneously to the beat of the music and Kasheef rolled down the windows to reintroduce the fresh air to his deprived lungs.

"Nigga, it's colder than a mu'fucka outside and you got the windows down!" Stick complained.

Kasheef smiled and said, "Yo', this might be one of the last times I get to smell air outside of the gates, nah mean?"

"Yeah, I feel you, fam," Stick replied. "So it's not looking good for you? That little slick bitch decided to snitch huh?"

"Yeah, fam. I just wish you could've handled that little job for me before she got the chance to talk to anybody," Kasheef mentioned.

Stick shook his head. "Yo', the way that chick got herself out of that was crazy. She walked right past us and into the arms of the cops, nah mean? But it's crazy though cuz she ain't snitch us out, so I was hoping she wouldn't have snitched you out and just kept her mouth closed."

"I don't know. I think I kind of forced her to talk by sending y'all at her," Kasheef admitted, remembering the message that Carmen had given on behalf of Alija.

"It's a shame, too, cuz shorty had a fat ass," Stick said while licking his lips. "I would have loved to get up in that."

Kasheef laughed and replied, "You wild li'l man."

The long car ride back to New York City gave Kasheef time to clear his head. He was livid with Norelle but he knew he had to approach the situation with her very carefully. She knew too much about him and the way he moved. He had introduced her to the streets and she was well aware of how he made his money. Whatever revenge he sought on her, it had to a surprise. If she knew he was out and gunning for her then she would try to hit him first, and there was a good chance that her blow may hurt worse than his. He also couldn't draw any attention to himself right now. Any negative publicity would hurt his case, so he couldn't take the risk of harming her physically. As they entered the city limits, Stick looked over at him and asked, "Are you going to the crib?"

Kasheef shook his head and replied, "Nah, I don't want Norelle to know I'm out yet. Ride by there though so I can peep something."

As they approached the Long Island apartment community where Norelle resided, Kasheef noticed a brand new Lexus sitting in Norelle's assigned carport. Kasheef smirked and nodded as he took in the gleaming black paint of the luxury coupe. *At least the bitch has good taste. I trained her well.*

If Kasheef had been any other man, Norelle's deception may have hurt, but Kasheef never let a woman get to close to his heart. It was one of the many reasons he'd never told Norelle that he loved her. He felt that he could only love something that was unflawed, and since no human could ever be perfect, he knew that to love someone would only be setting himself up for disappointment. His pride was wounded and his ego bruised, but his heart was intact. No tears, no lumps in the throat, or sharp pains in his stomach; his emotional state was unfazed. He would still, however, make sure that Norelle got what was coming to her. His ego would not allow him let it go. "Yo', you tryna make some quick paper?" he asked.

"You know I'm about my paper, fam; whatever it is, I'm with it," Stick replied.

"It's nothing big. Just tail her for a couple of days. I need to know what she's doing," Kasheef said curiously as he eyed the bedroom window of Norelle's place.

Stick replied, "Done."

Kasheef had Stick take him to a stash house that no one knew about. On the outside it looked to be abandoned, but the inside was modern and plush. It was one of several locations where he kept money. His major cash was secure in untraceable accounts, but he had hundreds of thousands of dollars that had not yet been washed, just laying around the city of New York. He pulled out $250,000 of dirty money. He reimbursed Stick for the bail money and gave him an extra ten stacks just because.

He then had Stick drop him off at a car dealership where he quickly dropped $50,000 on a Lincoln Navigator. He then swept the mall for some fresh gear, some personal essentials, and a cell phone. At the end of the night, he checked into the Marriott in midtown Manhattan on Lexington and Fifthy-first Street.

As soon as he walked into the room, he removed his clothes and hopped into the shower. He put his hands on the wall in front of him as he dropped his head and let the water caress his body. It had been almost a month since his arrest and he hadn't showered comfortably in a while. He had never been to jail before this, and now that he had been given a taste of what it was like, he never wanted to go back. His freedom was something that he had taken for granted, and if he was given a second chance, he decided that he was going to utilize it by getting out of the dope game.

Kasheef had been so accustomed to making fast money that he never got to enjoy it. His life had been a constant paper chase ever since he was a young boy, and it took for him to get locked up to realize that it was not how he wanted to live his life. He wanted to enjoy each and every day as if he would not see another sunrise. He needed to allow himself to feel again. The streets had hardened him and now he thought it was time for a change. He figured that he might open up a few businesses to give back a little bit of all that he had taken away by flooding the streets with heroin for so many years. He was only twenty-nine years old, but he was fourteen years strong in the game. Beginning his career as a hustler at age fifteen, he was seasoned and skilled at what he did. Over the years, he'd accumulated more than enough money to sit back and enjoy life. *All you've got to do is get through this trial.*

He closed his eyes and flashes of what happened the night of Mizan's murder graced his brain. He could see it clear as day. It was like someone had pressed play to a movie . . . only this movie was a true story. He could've tried the self-defense angle, but that would have been admitting that he'd actually killed a man, and he didn't think that a jury would be able to get past that fact, especially for a man like himself. Kasheef sighed and washed his body, staying underneath the stream of water until it turned cold. He thought of Alija and how afraid she had been the night of Mizan's death. He remembered how her body had shivered violently, and he shook his head as he recalled how he had let her go home that night when all along he had known he should have killed her. *I've got to talk to her. If she is serious about changing her statement I'll cash her out tonight.* He picked up his phone and dialed Carmen's number. He had to find out where Alija was staying.

"Hello?" Carmen answered, her voice filled with a husky sleep.

"Carmen, I didn't mean to wake you," Kasheef said as he glanced at the clock. It was a little past midnight.

"Kasheef?" she asked as she sat straight up in her bed.

"Yeah, it's me. I posted bail earlier today. Look, I need the address where I can find Alija," he said.

"Kasheef listen to me. I don't think it's wise that you go there. If anything happens to her you'll be the first person the police will—"

Kasheef cut her off. "I'm not going to do anything stupid, but I have to talk to her. I need to hear her proposition for myself." He heard silence fill the space between the phones. "Come on, Carmen. I need this. This is my life, ma."

A reluctant sigh filled the phone and Carmen closed her eyes. She knew what might happen if she gave away the information, but the sound of desperation in Kasheef's voice broke her down. She only hoped and prayed that Kasheef didn't do anything stupid. "Okay," she finally relented. "Okay, Kasheef. If you get caught or if anything happens to that girl, you didn't get her information from me."

"What information?" he asked, letting Carmen know he understood.

"She's at the Motel 6 in Long Island . . . room nine."

Kasheef hung up the phone, grabbed his keys, and rushed out of the room. He had some unsettled business to handle.

***

"Nahla? Baby, what's wrong?" Alija asked as she held her daughter and walked around the room, trying to calm her down. Her daughter had been crying all day and she was beginning to worry. What started out as whimpers of discomfort were now screams of pain, and Alija couldn't get Nahla to quiet down. "You can't be hungry," Alija said sincerely. "I just fed you." She checked Nahla's diaper. "And you're not wet."

Whaaa!

Whaaa!

The crying was so loud that Alija's eyes began to tear up in fear that something was seriously wrong with her daughter. She pulled out a thermometer from her daughter's diaper bag and checked her temperature. "A hundred degrees?" Alija said in confusion. She put her hand to her baby's forehead and, sure enough, Nahla was on fire. "Okay, La-La," Alija cooed, calling her daughter by her nickname. "Okay . . . We are going to get help right now," she promised as she slipped her daughter into her winter wear. She didn't even place her in her car seat; instead, she held her daughter against her chest, and grabbed the seat with her other hand as she headed out the door.

The crying was continuing to intensify. "I know, sweetheart, I know. Mommy's going to make sure everything is okay, don't cry." She ran to her car and strapped her daughter inside. She was moving so fast that her hands were shaking. She slammed the back door and ran around to the driver's door and hopped in, but when she went to turn her car over it wouldn't start. "No! Not right now! Please start!" she yelled as she hit her steering wheel. After trying for ten minutes straight, she decided to call an ambulance. She couldn't just let her daughter suffer, especially when she didn't know what was wrong. She jumped out of the car and grabbed Nahla out of the back seat.

A car pulled up behind her as she fumbled to unlock her motel room and balance Nahla all at the same time.

"Alija!" she heard a male voice call. She turned around and stared into the face of death himself . . . at least, of the man who had tried to bring death to her and her child.

"No!" she screamed as she began to bump her motel room door with her shoulder. She finally got the door open and rushed into the room, but before she could close the door, Kasheef had muscled his way inside.

"Please . . . please don't hurt me! I won't . . . ."

As soon as Kasheef saw the look in Alija's eyes, he instantly felt guilty. He could feel the fear radiating from her body. Her hands were shaking so violently that he was sure she would drop her child.

"Shh! Shh!" Alija whispered in her baby's ear as she backed away from Kasheef, putting the bed between them. "Please don't . . . ."

Kasheef put his hands up. "Calm down, ma. I didn't come here to hurt you," he said in his most convincing voice.

"Oh God, Nahla!" Alija cried. She was afraid for her life.

"Listen to me," Kasheef yelled in frustration. "I didn't come here to hurt you, Alija. I just want to talk."

Whaa!

"Yo', she doesn't sound good. Why is she screaming like that?" Kasheef asked.

Alija was reluctant to answer, but figured that if Kasheef had come to kill her, she would already be dead. "I . . . I don't know. She's been crying all day and she's running a temp. I was about to take her to the hospital, but my car . . . it won't start."

Kasheef approached Alija with his hands still raised in front of him for her comfort. "Give her here," he said as he took the baby from Alija's arms.

"No! Please . . ." Alija begged as she reached for her daughter.

"Look, get her shit together! I'm not about to do shit to you, girl! I'll drive you to a hospital," he stated with authority.

Alija nodded and grabbed the diaper bag. She went to her car and pulled out the car seat to transfer it to Kasheef's Navigator. Kasheef placed the child inside. "Get in," he told Alija.

She did as she was told, and Kasheef pulled off, burning rubber as he hit his gas in flight to the emergency room. Alija was silent. She couldn't believe that she was inside of Kasheef's car. She still didn't trust him, but he was her only hope of getting Nahla some help. When they arrived at the hospital, she jumped out and rushed her daughter inside.

"Help me! Please! There is something wrong with my baby," she told the nurse sitting behind the desk.

The nurse looked down at Nahla. By this time, her face had a bluish tint to it. "What's wrong with her?" Alija asked.

"Give her to me . . . we'll take care of her," the nurse said as she tried to pry the little body from Alija.

"No, I want to go with her," Alija cried.

Kasheef came up behind Alija and pulled her away. "Let them do their job, ma," he whispered in her ear. She let go, and cried as she watched them put her baby on a stretcher and wheel her through the emergency doors.

***

"She has lead poisoning and pneumonia?" Alija asked in disbelief as she sat beside her daughter's tiny bed in the hospital. "How? I mean, how did she get it?"

The doctor nodded and replied, "If she's been in an environment where there is old paint on the walls. Maybe a daycare, or restaurant, even your own home may have some old layers of poisonous lead-based paint on the walls. It can affect her immune system. She is young, so her lungs are not as resistant to infection as an adult's would be. Fluid can build up easily in an unsafe environment, especially in an area that is infected with lead."

"But she's going to be okay, right?" Alija asked.

"Yes. After a little bit of time, she is going to be fine. It is a good thing you brought her in when you did. If she'd gone overnight with that much lead in her blood she may have died." Just hearing those words made Alija cry out in pain. She couldn't imagine life without her daughter, and she had to take a minute to gain her composure.

"I'm sorry," she said as she wiped her nose with a tissue the doctor offered.

"It's quite all right, Ms. Bell. We'll keep Nahla for a couple weeks so that we can rejuvenate her lungs and immune system, but she will be perfectly healthy after that," the doctor said. "We do, however, need you to fill out your insurance information so that we can bill the company for her treatment."

"I don't have any—" Before Alija could finish her sentence, Kasheef, who had been standing near the doorway, interjected.

"We'll pay cash."

"Okay, then, the accountant at the front desk will take care of you," the doctor said. "I'll give you both a minute with your daughter, but visiting hours are over. You can't stay long."

Alija nodded and the doctor exited the room. Alija looked at her daughter and stroked her tiny hand. "Thank you, Kasheef. If it weren't for you . . ." she whispered without looking his way.

"You're welcome," he replied. They both stayed in the room for another half hour before the hospital staff came in to put them out. As promised, Kasheef paid Nahla's medical bills in advance, and then escorted Alija out of the building. When they were inside his truck he said, "I didn't come to hurt you tonight."

"Why did you send those dudes to my house to kill me?" she asked. "I wasn't going to say anything. I only went to the police after I felt my life was in danger."

"I apologize," he said as he drove through the city streets. "I was being selfish, trying to save my own neck."

"My daughter was in the house that night, Kasheef! I'll do anything to protect her," she said.

"I know. I realize that," he responded.

"How did she get lead poisoning?" Alija asked herself aloud.

"Probably that fucking rat hole you living out of," Kasheef commented.

"I was hiding out from you. It was all I could afford," she replied smartly as she rolled her eyes. She noticed that they were driving away from Long Island. She began to panic, and without hesitation she punched Kasheef in the side of his face.

"Aghh!" he bellowed as his hand went up to his right eye and his truck swerved. Alija kept swinging, until he pulled the car over and reached over to restrain her. "What the fuck is wrong with you, girl?" he asked.

"Where are you taking me?" she asked. "You're trying to kill me!"

"Girl, ain't nobody trying to kill your ass," he replied as he flipped up his sun visor and looked into the mirror at his damaged eye.

"Then where are we going?" she asked, breathing hard as she looked at him suspiciously.

"I was taking you to a better hotel. I didn't want you to have to take your little girl back to the same place where she got sick," he said.

"Oh," she said, feeling stupid.

"Yeah, oh, mu'fucka," he chastised. He shook his head and looked in his car mirror at his throbbing eye. "Sit ya' ass back," he said as he smirked at her. "I said I'm not going to hurt you."

She did as she was told and calmed down while he completed their drive. They pulled up to the same hotel where he was staying. He purchased another room and they rode the elevator to the twenty-first floor. Alija reluctantly followed him inside the room and he handed her the key.

"Make yourself at home. You can stay as long as you'd like. It's on my credit card so they'll just keep charging it until you check out," he explained.

She looked around the luxury room, and was grateful that he had checked her into a better environment. The 700 thread-count sheets and marble bathroom floors were a drastic change from the likes of Motel 6. "What did you come to my motel for? I thought you were still locked up," she said as she sat down at the table.

"I posted bail today. My lawyer came to see me about the offer you made. I wanted to talk to you about that," he said. "Are you really willing to go through with it?"

"Look, I don't want you to think I'm some money hungry hood rat, but I've got to look out for my daughter. She means everything to me, and you took what little security I had in my life away from me. If you pay me the money, I'll get up there and say that you are not the man who killed Mizan," she promised.

Kasheef stared at the girl and was reminded of how magnetic she had seemed the first night he had met her. The same night he'd shot Mizan. "Okay," he said.

"Okay?" she looked up in surprise.

"I'll pay you the money. I'm not trying to go to prison for the rest of my life. I know you saw what went down. It was either him or me, so I don't regret what I did. I am sorry you had to witness it, though," Kasheef said. "And I'm sorry about sending them niggas in your crib." His words were sincere in his apology because he meant everything he said. He made his way to the door. "I'll drop off the first half of the money tomorrow morning. You'll get the other half after you take the stand. I'm in 2106 if you need to get with me."

Alija nodded and smiled graciously as she walked him to the door. "Thank you, Kasheef . . . for not killing me, I mean," she joked.

"Thank you," he replied with a smirk as he pointed to the tiny black bruise she'd left near his eye. "For the black eye."

She closed the door behind him and a sense of relief washed over her body. She slid her back down the door until her bottom reached the floor. "Thank God," she whispered. "Now all I have to do is make it through this trial."

Chapter Ten

Alija slept comfortably in the lavish hotel room, and when the sun peeked through the curtains she didn't want to get up. It was the most rest she had gotten in a while and her body thanked her graciously for the change in atmosphere. The luxurious concierge room was significantly grander than the motel she had been hiding out in. She stretched her body as she yawned and slowly arose from the bed. Opening the curtains, she looked down onto the busy New York streets beneath her as sunlight streamed into her room. It was amazing to her how her life could be in shambles, yet everything in the world still ticked on normally as if she was not hanging onto her sanity by a thread. She wondered if any of the people below her could possibly have a life as complicated as her own. A knock at the door startled her and she turned to the intruding sound in annoyance. *It's only eight o'clock . . . Why is housekeeping knocking this early?* She went to answer it. She pulled the door open, ready to cuss somebody out, but to her surprise, Kasheef stood fully dressed and dapper as ever in hood gear.

"Good morning," he greeted warmly as he invited himself into the room. She pulled the hotel robe tightly around her frame and ran her fingers through her hair uncomfortably as he stared at her.

"What are you doing here? I . . . I mean, it's so early," she stammered.

Another knock at the door frightened her and she loo-ked at Kasheef in fear. She did not know what to expect from him yet, and the way he had sent a hit squad for her the first time she certainly would not put anything past him.

"You've really got to stop looking at me like that," he said as if offended. "You make me feel like the boogey man or some shit." He opened the door and in walked the concierge with a huge platter of food in his hands. He set it on the table, and Kasheef tipped him generously before he made his exit.

"I thought you might be hungry," he said as he sat down and pulled some of the plates in front of him.

"Hold on one second . . . I'm just going to freshen up," she said as she tiptoed to the bathroom. Staring at herself in the bathroom mirror, she frowned at her disheveled appearance. *I can't believe I was standing in front of him looking so crazy.* She washed her face, brushed her teeth, and pulled her hair up in a loose ponytail. When she exited the bathroom, she gasped at the sight in front of her. Her hand shot up to her mouth in shock.

"$100,000." Kasheef spoke calmly, as if that amount of money were chump change. The smug demeanor that he pos-sessed was as if he had been born among riches. It was obvious that he was accustomed to the finer things in life. He had spread the money all over Alija's bed, and laughed as she stood there, stunned beyond belief. It was the most money she had ever seen in her entire life. The hundred dollar bills wrapped in bundles were breathtaking. It was the most beautiful thing she had ever seen. She could not pick her jaw up from the floor.

"I, um . . . wow. Thank you," she whispered sincerely. That type of money could change her life. She had always been a girl form the hood. She had never aspired to be anything else, but the money in front of her could elevate her status and help her provide a new life . . . a new perspective for her family.

"Don't thank me. You are going to work for this cash, ma. You're about to make me look like a saint. I want you on the witness stand saying that I'm feeding starving kids in Africa," he said.

Alija laughed and Kasheef motioned toward the food. "Let's eat. You can tell me how you're going to spend my money."

Alija smirked at him, but she answered his question. "I'm going to take care of Nahla and get as far away from New York as I can. I just don't feel safe here anymore," she admitted. "You know how the hood views snitches."

"You don't have to worry about all that. You don't have to leave New York. I'll put it in the streets that you're good people," Kasheef stated.

"Thanks, but no thanks," she replied without hesitation. "I just need a new start. A new city for me and my baby. She is my everything."

"Where will you go?" he asked. "There ain't no better city than New York."

"Whatever you say," Alija answered sarcastically as she raised her brow in disagreement. "I'm going to Atlanta or somewhere else in the south, where I won't have to look over my shoulder every second of every day. It's slow and safe down there. I love my daughter and I don't want her to grow up here in the middle of the hood like I did." Alija smiled as she thought of her daughter growing up in a better place. "Nahla is my world."

"I can tell," Kasheef replied with a genuine smile.

"You got any kids?" she asked as she dug into Kasheef's pancakes. "You didn't order me none of these," she complained.

Kasheef laughed as he looked at the beautiful woman sitting across from him. As his eyes scanned her, he could not help but notice how attractive Alija was. She was the last person he expected to be cordial with, but now that he had met her formally, he was glad that he'd failed in his attempt to get her killed. He respected her. She was a good mother and a gorgeous young woman. His eyes discreetly roamed her toned arms and ample breasts that were easily visible through the satin camisole she was wearing. Her wide hips were complimented by a flat stomach, thick, juicy thighs, and defined legs. He looked down at her feet; even those were pretty. He felt like he was looking at a piece of art, her body was so well sculpted. "My fault, ma. Here, you can have these," he offered as he passed her the plate. "And, nah, I don't have kids. I haven't met anyone worth having them with. Most of these bitches out here don't need to be raising any kids anyway."

"Bitches?" she repeated in offense. She hated when niggas referred to women as bitches. It was so disrespectful. She did not doubt that Kasheef had come across many scandalous women, some of whom probably were hoes or bitches, but she felt like the lady a man chose showed who he really was. It took a bitch to know a bitch and a lot of bitch-ass niggas were choosing women who weren't shit because they themselves weren't shit.

"Yeah, ma, I'm not gon' hold my tongue. Most of these women out here are dirty," he stated as he thought of how Norelle had crossed him.

"I don't want you to take offense, but maybe you need to ask yourself why you keep attracting these dirty-ass 'bitches.' Maybe it's something about your dick that keeps these 'hoes,' coming around. I assure you that every woman ain't like that. Just the ones you fuck with," she defended as Kasheef reached to grab another bite of pancakes.

He chuckled at her logic and replied, "You've got a point."

She passed him the plate. "I'll share," she said. She looked at him and frowned as she remembered the visit she'd received from his girlfriend.

"What's with the look?" he asked. "You still don't trust me? You think I poisoned your food, ma?"

"No, it's not that. I have something to tell you," she said. He put down his fork and leaned back in his chair, ready to listen. She took a deep breath and continued. "I met your girlfriend."

"My girlfriend?"

"Yes, some girl named Norelle came to see me yesterday at the motel. She's grimy, Kasheef. She wants you to go away," Alija admitted.

"What did she say?" he asked. She knew that her words had struck a nerve because she could see his jaw clench as he gritted, his teeth.

"She offered to pay me $75,000 if I testified against you."

Kasheef shook his head. He couldn't believe that he had been sharing his bed with a woman like Norelle. He knew that she had deserted him and stolen his money while he was locked up, but to use his own money to pay off his witness was the ultimate betrayal.

"Take the money," he told her.

"What?"

"Take it. Tell her you're going to testify against me and take her cash. You can keep it. Use it for your daughter. When you get on the stand, do what we planned. Tell them I wasn't there. I'll take care of Norelle. She won't bother you," he assured her.

"Are you going to hurt her?" Alija asked. "Because if you are, I don't want no part of that. I have enough on my mind. I don't need to be feeling bad over a girl I don't even know."

"Did I hurt you?" he replied.

She shook her head, not really knowing if she believed him. They finished their breakfast in silence, and when they were done he reluctantly left, wishing that he could spend his entire day in her company. She was cool people and he enjoyed being around her. He almost felt like he had to make something up to her, make her life a little bit better, since he was the one who had ruined it in the first place.

***

Alija walked into the district attorney's office. She could not wait until this was over and her life returned to normal. She wished that she could get out of testifying all together, but there was no way that the state was going to let this case slip through their fingers willingly. Last night, she had seen a side of Kasheef that she did not know existed. He was a hustler, and she did not think men like him had hearts, but he had proven her wrong and shown her that there was more to him than met the eye. Oddly, she felt an allegiance to him. It was like they had become friends overnight. This trial had given them something in common; a bond between them that only they could understand. She had gone from fearing him to understanding him in only a few hours. Alija knew that she would have to be careful when dealing with him. His personality was magnetic, while his charm was seasoned and unpredictable. She did not want to get caught up in his world. She could not afford to. She had to force herself to remember that they were not friends.

"Hello, Alija," the DA greeted her.

"Hi . . . I don't mean to be rude or rush this process but I really need to make this quick. My daughter is in the hospital and I need to be with her," Alija stated.

Nancy Schwartz smiled understandingly. "Alija, I completely understand. This case is so open and shut, I can prosecute that murdering, drug-dealing bastard in my sleep. I really wanted to know how you were doing. We can't afford to let the defense trip you up. They'll try to distort your words, twist what you say, and make it seem as if you are unsure. Also, try to stay away from any reporters who try to speak with you. We don't need our star witness saying something that could jeopardize this case. If the public gets a hold of false information, it could be the death of my case. I have seen many cases go awry from people talking too much. Save all of your testimony for the courts. If you are okay with your testimony, and if you stick to what you told me and the police before, this entire process will run smoothly, okay?" The DA was almost 100 percent positive that she was going to win this case. She was confident in her ability. She didn't think that God Himself could change Kasheef's fate. She was going to make sure that he never saw the light of day again.

Alija nodded, "Okay." Alija left the office and headed straight to the hospital. She couldn't wait to hold her daughter. She was $100,000 richer and she could take care of Nahla. She was capable of giving her daughter the type of life she deserved, the life that she herself had never had.

She walked into her daughter's hospital room and was surprised to see pink balloons and yellow flowers throughout. She walked over to one of the bouquets and plucked the attached card.

> **To Baby Nala and Mom,**
> **Hopefully these flowers will brighten up your day.**
> **I hope you both feel much better today.**
> **You are very lucky to have one another.**
>
> **Kasheef**

Alija smiled because of the misspelling of her daughter's name, but knew that it was the thought that counted. She put the card back the same way that had she found it. She was appreciative of Kasheef's gesture, and a tear slipped down her cheek as she thought of what she was about to do. *Just get through this. Not much longer before all of this is over.* She went to her daughter's side.

"Hey, mama!" she said as she picked Nahla up. Her daughter reacted to her voice and opened up her eyes, but Alija was saddened to see that she was still very weak. The monitors that were hooked to her tiny frame broke Alija's heart. Her temperature was still elevated, but she knew that it would take awhile for Nahla to fully recover. "Well, let's see what mommy brought to entertain us today," Alija said. She reached into her diaper bag and pulled out a children's book. "The Cat in the Hat," she began. She opened up to page one and began to read aloud.

***

Kasheef didn't want to disrupt Alija as she read the book to her daughter. He was supposed to meet with Carmen today to go over his case, but after having the flowers and balloons sent to Nahla's room, he wanted to go check on her personally. The gentleness that Alija used with her daughter intrigued Kasheef. It was as if Alija lived only for Nahla. Their love was unlike anything he had ever encountered. Now that there was a possibility for him to go to prison, he desperately wished that he'd opened up his life to more affection. He was beginning to see that the only thing that had been missing in his life was what Alija had: pure love.

He stood with his arms folded against his white polo crew shirt until Alija was done with the story. It was crazy. She was the star witness against him, but he wanted to start a friendship with her all the same. He knew that everything would be ruined if they were seen together, but he was willing to risk it. He was just as infatuated with baby Nahla as he was with her mother. He had never seen such a beautiful little girl. Seeing a mother and daughter like them made him want a set of his own. In his eyes, a wife and child were the perfect accessories if you could find the perfect woman. But perfection was elusive, and he was not willing to settle for less, which was why he had yet to find his life partner. He cleared his throat to announce his presence, and Alija turned around in surprise.

"What are you doing here?" she asked sweetly.

"I just came by to check on Nahla," he said.

She stood up and placed her hands on her hips as if she was angry. "I can't believe you!"

"What?" he asked. *Yo', she be flippin' out on a nigga like she's my chick,* he thought as he touched his bruised eye gently and smiled slightly while shaking his head.

"You've known my daughter for an entire day," she said as she got up, grabbed the card, and pushed it into his chest, "and you don't know how to spell her name!"

She laughed when she saw the dumbfounded look on his face.

"Oh, you're trying to be funny," he said with a sexy smirk. "Keep ya' day job, ma."

She laughed and returned to Nahla's side. "No, seriously, thank you for the flowers and everything. She needs as much love as she can get."

"You don't have to thank me. I feel somewhat responsible, running you out of your home and all. How's she doing?" he asked.

"She still has a fever, but I think she'll be fine. The doctor said it will take a couple of weeks for her to recover, so I'm just putting it in God's hands," she replied.

"God? You trust Him that much?" Kasheef asked.

"You know what? I don't know. Before all this happened, I didn't think twice about God. I've never even been to church. It just feels like He's the only hope I have left," she replied.

"That's cool. I don't have faith in nobody but me. Trusting other people will get you fucked up," Kasheef said.

Nahla began to squirm and whimper, so Alija gently picked her up, making sure not to unplug any of the wiring. "You want to hold her?" she asked.

"Nah, I don't want to hurt her."

"Boy, sit down," Alija said playfully as she stood up so that Kasheef could take her place in the chair. She placed Nahla in his arms, and when her daughter stopped whining, her mouth dropped in an "O" of surprise. "Wow, she likes you."

"She's so damn small," Kasheef stated as he counted ten tiny toes and fingers.

Alija laughed at his ruggedness. Kasheef reminded her of someone she used to know. Her father had died when she was a small child, and the one thing she remembered about him was the way that he looked at her. He didn't look at her, he looked through her. He could tell if she was happy or sad, just by staring into her eyes. Her father could make the worst day better and he always made her smile. He was able to right any wrong, and fix anything that may have been broken, including her heart if it was ever shattered. Kasheef had the same gentleness about him. It was hidden underneath years of a rough visage, but she knew that it was there, beneath the skin. Inside his heart, Kasheef was just like her father. They were built alike, and she smiled at the distant memory.

"She's beautiful, Alija," he whispered gently as he stared at the little girl.

"Thank you," she replied.

Staring at the little girl was causing his insides to feel strange. Nahla's skin was soft as silk, her presence as cleansing as a confession, and her eyes as penetrating as a bullet. Holding the small child in his arms was the most innocent and trusting interaction that Kasheef had ever had. Baby Nahla was tugging at his heart. He had never seen anyone so precious, and he knew that after his name was vindicated, the first thing he was going to do was settle down and find the woman who could bring him the same joy that he felt right now. "Contact Norelle," he said as he stared at the child in his arms. "Get the money for your daughter. She deserves the best." With those words he handed Nahla back to her mother, then stood up and made his exit.

Chapter Eleven

"Dawn, can you get Kasheef Williams on the line for me?" Carmen asked, then released her intercom button.

A couple, minutes passed and then her phone line lit up. She picked up the call and said, "Kasheef! Why haven't you called me? What happened that night?" she asked eagerly, wanting to make sure Kasheef was not at risk for another murder charge.

"We're cool," Kasheef answered. "I've already paid her half of the money. She's game. I'm walking away from this . . . no bruises, no scratches."

"Okay, make sure you keep this quiet and stay away from Ms. Bell. She's still the enemy," she reminded him before hanging up.

Her hair upswept in a bun, she sat behind her desk with her legs crossed professionally at the ankle and tucked behind her. She inhaled deeply and let it out slowly to relax her mind. She was more at ease now that Kasheef had made the deal happen with the witness. She was still curious about Alija's background, however. Jumping into an arrangement like this was like having sex. She needed to know who she was getting in bed with, and it bothered her that she knew absolutely nothing about Alija. She hit her intercom.

"Yes, Carmen?" Dawn answered.

"Can you come in here please?" she asked.

A couple of minutes later Dawn entered the room.

"What have you found out about my Alija Bell?" Carmen asked as she removed her glasses and put them on top of her desk.

"Not a whole lot, really," Dawn replied.

"Oookay," Carmen said. "Be more specific."

"She has no record of criminal history. She's on government assistance and has one daughter. The birth certificate at the hospital was not signed by the child's father so that's a dead end. I tried to dig into her past and find out about her family, but I haven't had much luck on that either. It seems like I'm digging for a needle in a haystack. It would be much easier if I knew what I was looking for," Dawn admitted.

"I don't even know what I'm looking for," Carmen said.

"Do you think she's lying about witnessing the crime?" Dawn asked. She knew that she was not supposed to ask this, but the trial had garnered so much media attention that she could not help but find out the facts firsthand.

"Are you asking this off the record?" Carmen asked. She gave Dawn a skeptical look. She should not even have entertained the question, but the trial was driving her crazy, and having someone to talk to about it was like a release.

"Of course," Dawn replied.

"It doesn't seem like she is lying. She was there and she sounds pretty sure of what she thinks she saw. I just don't like surprises, you know?"

"Well, I'll keep digging, boss. If I find something that's even remotely suspicious I'll run it by you, and you can decide where you want to take it from there," Dawn suggested.

"Thanks, Dawn," Carmen said. "You're the best."

***

When Norelle received the phone call from Alija informing her that she was willing to deal with her, she was ecstatic. With that one conversation, Alija erased all worries from Norelle's heart. She sat in the parking lot of Motel 6 and waited for Alija to arrive. She hated this part of town and couldn't wait to pay Alija so that she could hightail it back to her fabulous life in the city. Checking her rearview and side mirrors continuously, she just felt like she would be robbed at any minute.

After today she would be home free. She planned on celebrating that night. There was no way anyone could talk her out of enjoying her riches and freedom. *Kasheef can rot his ass in the jail cell for all I care.* It was time for her to find a new man. It was out with the arrested baller and in with the new, upcoming hood star. She was indeed a hustler's wife. It didn't matter to her which hustler it happened to be, as long as his money was long and his name rang bells in the streets.

Norelle was relieved when she noticed Alija pull up behind her. She got out of the car and walked around to the passenger side of Norelle's car. She tapped on the window. Norelle unlocked her car doors so that Alija could hop in.

"Thanks for showing up," Norelle said.

"No, thank you for showing up," Alija replied. "Do you have the money?"

"So what are you going to say on the stand?" Norelle asked as she pointed to the oversized Gucci bag in the back seat.

"I'm going to tell the truth. I was there that night. I saw everything, and when I get on the stand, everyone in the room will feel as if they were there too. I may even shed a few tears," Alija laughed.

"A'ight, girl. Thanks for looking out. You know we women have to stick together," Norelle said.

"Like magnets," Alija answered. She unzipped the designer purse and saw stacks of money. "Is it all here?"

"Yeah, it's there," Norelle stated.

Alija opened the door and walked back to her vehicle. Once she was inside she watched Norelle drive away. "Stupid, stupid bitch," she mumbled as she tossed the money in her back seat. She headed back to the Marriott. She was feeling real thick. She now had $175,000 in her possession, all cash, and she still had more coming in once she testified. Feeling nostalgic and unable to contain herself, she palmed her cell phone from the table and called her sister.

"Mick, I need you to start working on that jury. Opening statements are tomorrow morning. Plant that seed early so that nothing goes wrong. At the end of the trial I'm going to break you off, a'ight?" she said.

"You know I got it on my end. Keep in touch," Mickie replied.

"I will, but not too much. There is so much riding on this. Let's not get sloppy. We don't want to get caught," she reminded her sister. "Just stick to the plan."

***

"Yo', Sheef, Norelle just left Motel 6," Stick reported as he tailed her, staying two car lengths behind.

"What she been doing?" Kasheef asked.

"Nothing really; spending up all your dough like crazy. I've been seeing her around that nigga, Fiasco," Stick reported.

Kasheef felt his blood boil at the mention of Fiasco's name. He was a new cat who had come into New York from the Midwest a couple of months back. He had come around to shake things up since Kasheef's arrest. He knew that Kasheef could not make a move of retaliation because it would draw attention to his case. Norelle was getting out of pocket by messing with his adversary, and he wanted to smack the taste out of her mouth for breaking the code.

"Fiasco, huh?" Kasheef seethed anger through every word as he gritted his teeth. He wasn't bothered by Norelle messing with another man. He was hot because of the way that she went about it. She was disrespectful and was now associating with the enemy. "What else is she doing?"

"She just gave ol' girl a big ass purse though."

"Okay, stay on her. I'ma let her see my face tonight. See what she got to say for herself, nah mean?"

"She gon' shit a ton of bricks," Stick shouted with laughter in his voice. He would have paid to see the look on her face. "You want me to handle her since you under so much heat?"

"Nah, fam. I got something else planned for her. That's love though, baby. Good looking out," Kasheef responded. "Get at me when she's on her way to crib later on tonight. I need to know when to show up."

"One." Stick disconnected the call with a twisted smile on his face.

***

Norelle couldn't contain herself. She had dropped off the money, and now her future was secure and her fate was in her own hands. With a safe full of money, she felt accomplished. It didn't matter to her that she had swindled her way to the top. She called Carmen and asked if she wanted to meet her for drinks. They decided to meet at the 40/40 club in Manhattan. Norelle stayed dressed to impress, so there was no need for her to stop and change. She was slowly becoming a diva and socialite on Kasheef's expense.

She walked into the club with a newfound independence. Since Kasheef had gone away, she did feel lonely, but she knew that money was harder to attain than men, so she felt that the switch was worth it. Kasheef was easily replaceable; money was not.

As she sat down at the bar, she noticed Carmen walk through the door. Stepping into the popular club wearing a cream Fendi pencil skirt and ruffled blouse, Carmen was dressed just right for the occasion. Her fashionable appearance fit right into the upscale atmosphere of the club. Hood fellas and businessmen alike, who were working with major chips, all turned their heads to get a peek at Carmen's backside as she sashayed by.

Norelle smiled as Carmen approached, and they kissed each other once on each cheek before taking their seats. Norelle had just become reacquainted with Carmen, so she decided to keep her recent actions concealed from her. She didn't know how she would react, and she definitely didn't want Kasheef to find out. With Carmen being Kasheef's lawyer, she knew that it would be a conflict of interest. She also did not need Carmen to pass judgment on her. Norelle knew what she was doing was wrong, but to her it was worth it. She did not need random opinions of people trying to tell her how to live. She was going to do her regardless; right or wrong.

"Hey!" Norelle shouted over the loud music.

"How have you been holding up?" Carmen asked.

"I'm good. Real good actually, but can you do me a favor and not talk about Sheef's case tonight? I just need a break from it all," Norelle insisted.

Carmen nodded. "I understand."

Stick entered the club and spotted Norelle sitting at the bar next to Kasheef's lawyer. He walked to the bar, knowing that Norelle would never recognize him. Kasheef kept his women separate from his friends. They were the treasure everybody wanted, but no other man could get to. Kasheef was smart; he never gave another man the opportunity to get in his woman's ear, and now Stick was glad that they had never met. He took a seat directly next to the two women and ordered a drink from the bartender. He pretended to blend in with the crowd as he listened to the conversation going on next to him.

"I bought a new place," Norelle said.

"Really? Where?"

"It's in the city, in a building near Union Square. I just need a change. It doesn't feel right sleeping in my old place. The police turned it upside down and it just doesn't feel like home anymore. I had furniture delivered there today. I just want to forget about the past and move forward," Norelle said making up a small white lie. "As a matter of fact, I think I may sleep there tonight."

Stick pulled out his cell phone and sent a text message to Kasheef:

Ya' girl bought a place near Union Square. She's going there tonight; I'll tail her to find out the exact address.

***

Kasheef received the text message and knew exactly where Stick was referring to. He did not need Stick to tell him where it was located. Norelle had shown him the vacant condo a couple of months ago, and he had been considering buying it as a birthday gift for her. He shook his head in contempt and headed toward his destination. Norelle was showing an entirely different side of herself. He had known that she had her faults, but she had turned out to be a complete snake.

When he arrived, he looked up toward the luxury building as he parked his car across the street. He knew that Norelle would be shocked to see him, and he was well aware of the temptation he had to break her neck. He urged himself to remain calm. He had to do this right. What he had in store for Norelle was much worse than death. He just had to be patient.

***

Norelle stumbled into the elevator. She was a bit tipsy from all the cocktails she had consumed while at the club. It was the first night that she would spend at her new apartment, and the first thing she wanted to do was peel out of her clothes and enjoy her Jacuzzi-style bathtub. She opened the door and stepped into the apartment. Darkness and unfamiliarity enveloped her, and she ran her hands along the walls as she searched for a light switch. When she finally found one, the high ceilings and hardwood floors were illuminated. She walked down the narrow hallway and into the living room, and gasped when she saw a male figure sitting on her brand new furniture.

"Who are you? What are you doing in my house?" she asked. The man didn't respond. "I'm calling the police." Norelle ran toward her door, but stopped mid-step when the man spoke.

"I didn't know you were buying a new crib," Kasheef said slowly, calmly.

"Kasheef?" she asked. Her nerves got the best of her and she began to stutter. "Wh . . . when did you get out? Why didn't you call me to let me know you were home?" she asked nervously as she backed up toward the front door. She knew that she was caught. Here she was buying condos and cars while she was telling her man that she didn't have the money to bail him out. She was busted; now all she could do was run for her life.

Kasheef stood up and walked over to Norelle. "You planned on leaving me?"

Norelle opened her mouth to explain, but no words came out.

"Huh?" Kasheef asked in a whisper. His low tone was almost more menacing than his yell, and the look in his eyes sent shivers up Norelle's spine. "You were just gon' leave me in there?" He approached her until her back was against a wall. He put his hands around her neck and rubbed gently as he stared her in her eyes.

She closed her eyes and flinched from the unexpected.

"You afraid of me now?" he asked.

She nodded truthfully, but didn't open her eyes. She saw her life flash in front of her. She couldn't understand it. *How the hell did he get out without me knowing about it? Why didn't Carmen say anything?* Kasheef's face was inches away from her own. He was so close to her that she could smell the peppermint scent of his breath. "I'm sorry," she stammered.

"I know why you did what you did," he said as he backed away from her.

Norelle was confused, and speechless.

"Please come sit down with me and talk," Kasheef said as he took a seat on her plush leather sofa and patted the cushion next to him.

Reluctantly, Norelle obliged and sat down near him, being sure to leave a bit of space between them just in case he decided to pounce on her.

"All of this is my fault," he continued. "I know what type of woman you are, Norelle. I know you better than you know yourself. You are high maintenance. You live to be on top. Everything that I've provided you with over the years, you deserved. I knew when I met you that you were not attracted to me. You were attracted to what I could give you. What I could do for you, nah mean?"

"That's not true," Norelle whispered back, attempting to keep up her façade.

"You ain't got to lie to me, ma. I know your game and I respect it. You had your use for me. It was the money. I provided you with a lifestyle. Me, I also had my use for you. You were my trophy. You were the woman I stepped out with when I wanted to shine," he said as he lifted Norelle's chin from her chest with his finger.

She smiled slightly, but was still unsure. "So you're not mad at me? Because I swear, Sheef, I'll pay you back every dime," she promised quickly. "I just didn't know what to do. I never thought you would go to jail."

"I'm not gon' lie to you; when you first left me stinking up at Rikers, I was hot. That shit had me tight, but it's not important anymore. I'm out and I understand. See, even though we were using each other, something happened to me while I was with you. You stole my heart, ma," he whispered smoothly. "So even if I go away, I still want to make sure you're straight. I know you were just worried about you. You didn't know how you were going to survive, but I'll never leave you stuck like that. I want you to be okay and financially set even if I go away," Kasheef explained.

"I don't know what to say, Sheef," Norelle replied. "I just wish you had told me before I did all of this. Now you will never trust me again." Norelle really didn't have any remorse for what she had done, but she was for damn sure going to play this new role he had assigned her. The way he was talking, he was going to make sure she was okay for the rest of her life and she was going to cooperate in order to get more money. *I slipped up this time, but once Alija testifies, the jury will find him guilty. When I'm sure he's in jail for life I'll drop him like hot grease.*

"Let's not worry about that," Kasheef stated. "I just want to enjoy the little bit of time that I have left with you. Just in case I lose in court, I want to make each moment count."

Norelle hugged Kasheef in complete disbelief at how naïve he was. *I would have been hustling his ass if I knew it was going to be this easy.* Kasheef gripped her waist tightly and then pulled away from her and said, "Look, before I go in, I'm going to hit you off with a lot of money. Don't keep in it the house. Stick up kids gon' automatically assume that I left you with my stash, so it won't be safe to keep it here. Tomorrow morning I want you to go and open up a bank account. I'll make sure you have something to put in there, a'ight?"

"Okay, Sheef," she replied as she took his face in her hands. "I love you."

"I know you do." Kasheef hugged her and frowned. He found it funny how the words "I love you" could slip out of her mouth so easily. It was because of women like her that he did not believe in love. Women like Norelle made it hard for him to believe that love really existed because they lied on love's behalf so easily, as if it meant nothing. He pulled away and headed for the door. "I've got to go."

"Wait!" she yelled. "Why won't you just stay here?"

"I don't want you to be involved in any of this drama. The first day of my trial begins tomorrow. You'll be better off if we keep our distance. I'll come and check on you, though. Call me after you open the account. I'll have the money for you in a couple of days," he said.

Norelle blew him a kiss and Kasheef left without responding. It had taken all that he had not to choke the air out of Norelle's lungs. He was just happy that he had not lost his top. Revenge was so much sweeter when it was unexpected.

Chapter Twelve

"Hello, ladies and gentlemen of the jury. Over the course of this trial, the defense is going to use a barrage of illusions to trick you into freeing a guilty man," Nancy Schwartz began her opening statement, while leaning on the jury box and pointing one finger toward Kasheef. "They will hold no punches as they try to paint a lovely portrait on a dilapidated, cold, brick wall. They may even try to bring up the past of a little boy raised in an urban environment who had no choice but to adapt to his surroundings. Let me put this question in your mind before all of this even begins. What does any of that have to do with a murder? Upbringing, charity contributions, or any other tool that the defense tries to use has nothing to do with murder. They are just distractions. Good distractions, I might add. As a matter of fact, let's give a preemptive round of applause to the defense right now for their creativity." Nancy Schwartz walked straight over to the defense table and stood directly in front of Kasheef. She clapped her hands loudly before turning her attention back to the jury. "You see, ladies and gentlemen, Ms. Rose here is a very skilled magician, who has made many charges disappear for many known criminals."

Carmen smirked, but did not interrupt. She knew that the DA would be pulling out all stops in trying this case. This was Carmen's first big case, and the DA was trying to make it seem like Carmen had defended John Gotti or someone. Nancy

Schwartz was declaring war on Kasheef and she wanted to draw first blood. She wanted to be inside of the heads of the jurors, but she would have to do much better if she wanted to intimidate Carmen. Carmen tapped her pen against the desk and listened on.

"Don't let her turn this trial into another one of her magic shows. Over the next couple of weeks, the state will present you with the facts. We will give you an eyewitness' account of what occurred on the night of March 21, 2008. A courageous young woman, who can identify the killer of Mizan Simmons, has agreed to share with you her account of what happened that night. There can only be one person to blame, and the state will prove that person to be Kasheef Williams. Mr. Williams is the one responsible for the murder. It is his fault that a little girl will grow up without a father. It is his fault that a mother had to bury her son. It was at his hands that this tragic murder took place, and now it is in your hands to bring him to justice. It is your responsibility to right this wrong." District Attorney Schwartz gave Kasheef a smug look before she took her seat. Kasheef shifted uncomfortably in his chair.

He leaned over to Carmen, "Who the fuck is she looking at like that?"

Carmen grabbed his arm and squeezed it gently. "Don't worry about it. I got this."

Kasheef turned around and scanned the crowd. Norelle sat directly behind him as if it were her place to be by his side. He gazed past her when he noticed Alija sitting in the last row of the room. He winked his eye and saw her smile, then turned back around.

It was Carmen's turn to deliver her opening statement. She was a woman determined as she approached the jury looking fly as ever. Her long, tailored, tan Dolce pencil skirt, a high-rise design, stopped right below her bust line. She wore a silk tan blouse with a ruffled neckline and a sleeveless tan vest to accent her outfit. Her Giuseppe stilettos click-clacked against the floor as she walked.

"Hello, ladies and gentleman of the jury, how are you all doing today?" she asked with a genuine smile. She decided to take the lay-back approach with her jury of mostly women. She quickly scanned the faces of the jury. Two white women, five black women, one Hispanic woman, three white men, and one black man could either make or break her entire career. All that she had worked hard for was riding on this.

"I am here to set the record straight. Mr. Kasheef Williams is not a criminal, nor is he a threat to our society. In fact, the DA is right. He has contributed thousands of dollars to local charities and even political figures. In fact, I believe Mr. Williams contributed $50,000 to Judge Martin's campaign when he was up for judicial election." Carmen turned toward the judge, who turned beet red at the public revelation. Several members of the jury chuckled, and Carmen continued. "He's never been in trouble a day of his life. It seems to me like he would work his way up to something as big as murder!" she said incredulously. "You know? Give him a little bit of practice. Maybe commit a couple robberies, get himself an aggravated assault charge . . . something. Murderers are not made overnight," she argued.

"Kasheef Williams is a law-abiding citizen who does not have the stealth or the malice in him to commit a crime of this magnitude. He's had no practice. No priors whatsoever. He is simply the wrong man, and while the state is here wasting your tax dollars, the real killer is roaming free around our city streets. The district attorney can call me a magician and try to put all of these biases into your heads to help her case, but the truth is I represent the underdogs. I speak for those who can not speak up for themselves; the men and women who would otherwise be trampled on and punished for crimes that they were not responsible for. All I'm asking you is to keep an open mind while you are hearing this case. Don't let the state make your decision for you. This is someone's future you are playing with. Be 100 percent sure that the man before you is your murderer. If you feel like he's the perpetrator of this crime, then by all means, convict him. If you have even the slightest sliver of doubt that leads you to believe that something just doesn't quite add up, then you are obligated by law to let my client go. None of my so-called magic is needed here. The only thing I need from you, ladies and gentleman, is an open mind. An open mind is all you need to render a fair and just verdict. I can assure you that Mr. Williams is innocent. Now I just have to get you all to see the innocence in this man that I see."

The first day of the trial went by quickly. Both sides went through the coroner's report of the body. The short man sat on the stand and gave a detailed account of the decomposition of Mizan's body once it had been recovered from the river. The prosecution used gory details to horrify the jurors and played the sympathy card by reminding them of the family that Mizan had left behind. Carmen could tell that Kasheef was concerned about the effect that the coroner was having on the jury, because his body was tense and his usually calm demeanor was now anxious as he tapped his foot against the floor.

When it was time for cross-examination, Carmen arose from her seat and walked over to the coroner. "Was there any evidence left on the body that would indicate that Mizan Simmons contributed to his own death?" Carmen asked.

"Well, there was a small trace of gun powder on the deceased's hands," the coroner replied.

"So the victim was not as heroic and innocent as the

prosecution is making him out to be. There are no gun permits registered in Mizan Simmons' name. So it may be safe to say that the shooter, whoever he maybe, could have been protecting him or herself from the deceased," Carmen said.

"That is very possible," the coroner replied.

"No further questions, Your Honor," Carmen said, and then returned to the defense table.

Both sides went back and forth for a few hours before court ended for the day. Kasheef, exhausted and more worried than ever, retired to his hotel room for the remainder of the day. He lay in bed with his hands behind his head. He thought of his trial as he felt the stress build in his shoulders. He couldn't ask for a better lawyer. Carmen was great and was doing a damned good job, but there was only so much that she could do. The prosecution had it out for him. They portrayed him to be this horrible monster and he could see their words taking their toll on the jury already. They wanted a bad guy and Kasheef was it.

A small knock at the door interrupted his thoughts and he walked somberly over to it. When he opened it up, Alija stood before him in a black BCBG jogging suit that hugged every curve of her voluptuous body.

"Hi," she said in a low voice. "I just came to check on you. I could tell by the look on your face that you weren't happy in there today. I thought you could use a friend." Alija smiled half-heartedly as she looked up at Kasheef.

Kasheef moved to the side to let her in, but peeked his head into the hallway to be sure no one had seen her come to his room.

"Don't worry, I made sure I was low key," she said, knowing that they were not supposed to be associating with each other. "Now, what was wrong today? Tell me what's on your mind."

"They are trying to put the noose around my neck."

"Why are you so worried?" she asked. "You have the entire thing in the palm of your hands."

"I know, but when I'm sitting in that courtroom I feel
like I'm choking," he admitted. Being vulnerable in front of other people was something that Kasheef did not do often. He was
surprised that he was opening up to Alija in the way that he was.
"How's li'l mama doing?"

"She's good. I went to see her after I left the court house.
She's still not ready to come home, though."

He walked over to sit down on his bed. With his face
buried in his hands, he sighed deeply. Alija was shocked at this
new connection she felt with Kasheef. He was her enemy, but
here she was in his room. She was beginning to view him as
one of the only friends she had. One of the only people who
could understand what she was going through. *If he only knew,*
she thought regretfully. She sat down next to him. "Everything
will be fine. We just have to get through this. Once this is over
we can go our separate ways," she said.

"What if I don't want that?" he asked as he turned his
head to look at her.

Tears filled her eyes and she willed them away, but
didn't respond. She wrapped her arms around herself as if she
were cold. "I don't think you know what you want, Kasheef. Not
long ago you wanted me dead . . . now you're saying you want
me here with you? I think you're just alone right now and you
think that I'm what you are looking for. You just found out all
that stuff about your girlfriend and you are searching for a quick
replacement; someone who you can trust. Or maybe you just
want to play with my head and get involved with me because
of our agreement. I don't know what is up with you, but if you
think I am who you want or what you want in a woman, believe
me, I'm not. You have no idea who I am. You don't know any-

thing about my past or what I'm capable of. I will be nothing but heartbreak for you."

"I've been alone my entire life, ma. I just see something in you. When I look at you, I respect you and I have never felt that way about anyone. I can kick it with you, nah mean? I see you with your daughter and it just feels right. It all feels right when I'm with you," he admitted.

"But it would be so wrong," Alija whispered as she touched Kasheef's face. If it had been under different circumstances, she may have given him a chance, but the way that their paths had crossed would forever haunt her. She just could not take it there. She could not allow herself to. "I have to be honest with you. You scare me. Just the way that we met and—"

Kasheef cut her off. "I would never hurt you."

"My heart seems to know that. I mean, for these past few days you have been the only person I can talk to, but my mind . . . my mind is telling me that not too long ago, you wanted me dead. What if I had not gotten away from your goons that night?" she asked as she stared into his face. "I would be dead and quite possibly my daughter would be dead."

The way Kasheef looked at her as she spoke caused her to blush. He stared at her so intensely that she had to break his gaze. He intimidated her. "That was then," Kasheef whispered as he brought his face toward hers. She pulled away, he pulled her back . . . taking control of her, commanding her to come nearer until their lips touched. He kissed her slowly. "Now I'll kill anybody who tries to bring harm to you," he said as her gently sucked her bottom lip into his mouth.

Alija resisted, putting her hands up against his chest and pushing him away. "No, this isn't right . . . you're not for me," she whispered, but the softness of Kasheef's full lips drew her back in each time she pulled away.

"I'm sorry, ma," he said to her repeatedly as he kissed her smoothly, his voice like a classic melody to her ears as she gave into him with regret. "I'm sorry . . . I need you. Don't tell me no."

Aljia's heart raced as she returned his kisses passionately, their tongues intertwining like a slow dance. "Kasheef," she moaned, knowing that she should stop. This was not a part of her plan. He was getting to her, and he was a completely different person than what she had first expected.

"Shh!" he said as he pulled her shirt over her head. His kisses trailed from her mouth to her neck to her hard, dark pearls as he moved from one breast to the other, circling her erect nipples with his tongue as he palmed them softly.

Alija's back arched and Kasheef stood, then picked her up. She wrapped her legs around his waist. The womanly crease between her legs was soaked in anticipation. Kasheef's hands massaged her round behind and his fingertips melted into her skin, causing a wave of pleasure to pulsate through her body. He put her on her feet and reached down into her pants. When he brought his fingers out they were dripping wet. "Do you want me to stop?" he asked.

"Yes," she said as she backed toward the door. Kasheef watched her walk away, and as she turned to open the door he came up behind her and closed it, pinning his body against hers.

"Don't leave, ma," he whispered in her ear, then planted kisses on the back of her neck. She closed her eyes, her hand still on the door handle. "Make love to me, ma."

"No," she answered softly, her eyes closing as she felt his hands on her body.

"Stay," he coaxed.

"No," she moaned as she felt his hand palm her soaking love box through her jeans. It felt so good that her breath caught in her throat.

"Yes," he whispered as he turned her around, looking her in her steamy bedroom eyes. "Say yes."

"No," she whispered as she reignited their kiss.

Kasheef removed her pants and picked her up by her behind, her legs wrapping around him again.

"Say yes for Daddy," he commanded.

"Yes," she finally moaned. He lay her down on the bed, where she spread her legs and invited him into her warmth. He filled her up with ease. Her walls contracted against the width and size of his manhood. Her fingernails dug into his back as their bodies moved in unison to an inaudible beat. Kasheef rolled into her gently, and she matched him thrust for thrust.

He admired her while he sexed her body. He had never had a sexual experience like the one he was having right now. His emotions were attached to his actions. He felt something for Alija, and because he had never loved another person in his life he could not say that love was what he was feeling. He just knew that it was different. It was better.

He kissed her nose, her forehead, her collarbone; any place that his eyes graced his lips followed. She was perfect. Every inch of her body, of her soul, of her heart was perfect. It wasn't that she was without flaws, but he was blind to them. She had a few stretch marks here and there just like every other chick in America, and her attitude could match that of a lioness, but to him these things were flawless. He did not want to change a single thing about her. To another man she may not have been the total package, but Kasheef was finally realizing that when you find the one person who was built for you, you are blind to their imperfections. Alija was the perfection and companionship that he had been searching for his entire life. The same way that he had fallen in love with her baby daughter while she was sick in the hospital, he was falling in love with Alija, who was now beneath him in his bed.

Their passion intensified. A slow grind became a fast pace as their carnal passion took control. Kasheef felt the tension building up in his toes.

Alija moaned, "Kasheef, I'm cumming."

"Me too, ma, me too," he whispered as he plunged in and out of her honey pot while she dug her nails deep into his muscular behind. "Ooh shit," he whispered. Alija had to have the best pussy ever. He closed his eyes and slowed down while going in as deep as his tool would take him.

"Kasheef!" she moaned as her body shuddered. He felt her warm, womanly fluids break through her dam and flood onto his shaft. The feeling was so incredible. It was so warm and wet that he reached his peak and came with her.

Exhaustion wreaked her body and Alija inhaled deeply as she tried to catch her breath. She could not believe what she had just done. The heat of the moment had taken her life in a direction she had never anticipated. She could feel a tear slide down her cheek, and Kasheef wiped it away while looking her into her eyes. They were deep with emotion, and he felt as if he could stare at her forever.

He opened his mouth to speak, but Alija silenced him with her finger. She shook her head and said, "Don't. Don't say anything to ruin the moment. Just hold me. We've only known each other for a few days . . . so this can't be real . . . so please don't say anything. Just be here in this moment."

Kasheef couldn't stop staring into her eyes. He felt lost, and in her eyes he found the path that he should take. He lay down and brought her into his arms. Just being in the same room with Alija was like playing with fire. If the state knew that the two had been in contact, they would charge him with witness intimidation, and no matter what Alija said on the stand, people would think he coerced her testimony. Kasheef could feel the rise and fall of her chest as she breathed deeply. The rhythm of her heartbeat was soothing to his damaged soul. He didn't know what she was thinking or what would become of them, but he did know that he cared for the woman lying in his arms, and if he had his way he would never let her go.

***

Daylight came peeking through the curtains of the hotel and Alija stirred from her peaceful slumber. She was still wrapped in Kasheef's arms and she reluctantly slid from underneath him. *What am I doing?* she thought frantically. *I'm not supposed to catch feelings for this man. Where are my clothes?* She found her belongings neatly folded and placed inside one of the drawers of the armoire. She tiptoed as quietly as she could around the room, and slipped into her outfit from the night before. Finding a pen and paper on the nightstand, she left Kasheef a note.

I can't do this with you. I wish that I could, because no man has ever made my body feel the way that you did last night, but it is not right. I know that you don't understand, but just trust me. Everyone involved would just end up getting hurt.

She didn't sign her name, and left the note on the vacant pillow in Kasheef's bed. She kicked herself all the way to her room. Now she would have to keep her distance from Kasheef. She had to admit that it was hard to deny his charm. There was a swagger about him that lured her in. Every time she was around him she felt jittery, like a schoolgirl who had a huge crush, but she couldn't fall in love . . . not with Kasheef. She picked up her cell phone and dialed Mickie's number. Her sister answered on the first ring.

"Where have you been?" Mickie asked. "I came by the motel to make sure everything was all right and you weren't there!"

"I checked out of the motel. I'm in a hotel in midtown," Alija explained.

"Midtown?" Mickie questioned. "Bitch, where did you get Midtown money from?"

"Never mind all that. You're not supposed to be coming to see me, Mick! Don't fuck this up!" Alija yelled the words as she sobbed into the phone. She was overwhelmed, and she just needed her life back.

"Whoa! What the hell is wrong with you?" Mickie asked.

"Nothing, Mick. I'm sorry. I'm just tired of all of this, you know?" she asked. "I called you to tell you to make sure the jury was still on track. You don't have any individuals trying to have their own opinions, do you?"

Mick smacked her lips and replied, "Girl, since when have I ever given anybody the option to have their own damn point of view? I got this. Unless you tell me differently, the jury is going to do what I say."

"Okay, good. After this is over we are all going to be a lot richer. Kasheef is going to pay me the money after I testify," Alija said. "So just hold on, Mick."

"A'ight, girl. I love you."

"Love you too," Alija answered, and then hung up the phone.

***

Kasheef read the note and crumpled it in his hands. He was aware of the fear that he had instilled in Alija, but he was positive that he could erase the negative connotations that she had formed in her mind regarding him. She needed time, but that was something that he was not guaranteed. He had to have her now.

Kasheef arose from the bed and showered quickly. Court was due to reconvene in a few hours, and he had some business he needed to handle before he met up with Carmen. Clad in formal Sean John apparel, the black suit and Steve Madden shoes distinguished him. At six feet three inches, he hung a suit quite well. He went to visit his accountant who managed his money, and made sure that it was kept securely overseas. He wanted to make sure that all of his accounts were undetected by the IRS. The last thing he needed was a tax evasion charge to add to the stresses he was already dealing with. After being sure that his money was protected, he headed for Norelle's condo.

He knocked on the door and was greeted with a smile as Norelle pulled him into her home. "Hey, you! What took you so long to come and check on me? I have been missing you," she said. Kasheef could see how he had been blind to her true intentions. Norelle was a great actress and never broke out of character. Even now she was still acting, pretending to care for him. She was indeed a beautiful liar.

"I had a couple of things that needed to be taken care of," he answered. "Come take a ride with me."

Norelle grabbed her clutch purse and followed him out of the apartment. "Where are we going?"

He put his hand on the small of her back and led her to the car. He opened the passenger side door and guided her inside. "To handle this business," he responded. "You saw how the prosecution did me yesterday. I may be going to prison and I want you to be straight. I got the money in the back seat. I'm about to take you to a bank so that you can open yourself an account and deposit it." He made sure that he was sincere in his tone. He wanted her to trust him, and, naively, she did. *Money hungry bitch,* he thought as he got in his car and pulled away from the curb. He took her to a Chase bank, pulled curbside, and said, "Go ahead."

"You're not coming in? I don't even know how much money this is," she said.

"Nah, ma, I can't come in there with you. I'm under investigation so we don't want anybody to think that this is my money. You have to do this yourself so that you will have no traces to me. This is your cash now," he said as he leaned in and kissed her lips. "I just want to take care of you."

She smiled and kissed him back. "I'll be back in a minute," she said as she took the briefcase out of the back seat and headed into the bank.

I can't believe how stupid he is, she thought as she sashayed into the bank. She walked to the reception area where she was greeted by a banker.

"Hello, how can I help you?" he asked.

"Yes, I'd like to open an account," she said as she set the briefcase down and popped it open, revealing the money that lay neatly inside. The banker's eyes opened wide, and he motioned for her to come into his office. Norelle didn't hear much of what the banker explained to her. The only thing she kept thinking about was the new life she would lead once Kasheef was locked up. After giving the banker her personal information like address and social security number, they counted the money, which totaled $400,000. She intended on adding the rest of the money that she had originally stolen from Kasheef's safe, and would have more than a half million dollars. A wicked grin crossed her face as she shook hands with the eager banker. She walked back out to the car, where Kasheef waited with his seat leaned back and one hand propped on the steering wheel.

"You get it done?" he asked.

"Yeah, it's all taken care of," she replied. She hopped into the car and he pulled away, satisfied that everything had gone off smoothly. The $400,000 was a huge chunk of what he had acquired in the streets. In all, he had $2 million stashed in his accounts. He had given Norelle all of the money that he had not washed yet. He still had product on the streets, which had the potential to earn him more revenue, but he wouldn't be able to touch that for a while. He planned on putting Stick on to his connect. After he beat this case he was going to retire and enjoy some of the dirty money he had made over the years.

***

"Are you ready?" Carmen asked.

Kasheef looked around the crowded courtroom. Cameras flashed in his eyes and spectators whispered speculative comments regarding his arrest, but he ignored it all. He was looking for someone in particular. He was hoping to see Alija in the back row, but she wasn't there. Her absence caused a dampening spirit to overcome him.

"Kasheef?" Carmen called his name to get his attention. "Is everything all right?"

"Yeah, everything's fine," he replied as he focused his attention toward the judge who was now entering the room.

"All rise!" the bailiff announced. "The honorable Judge Campbell Martin presiding."

"Be seated," the judge said.

The day's events began with the prosecution. The district attorney arose from her seat, and one of her paralegals rolled a television stand to the middle of the room, facing it toward the jury.

"Yesterday, the defense and I bantered back and forth. You heard a lot of speculation and hearsay as to what occurred the night Mizan Simmons was shot dead. Everyone wants to know what really happened that night. The tape that you are about to view will answer all of those questions. You will see it with your own eyes," she said. She bent down and pressed play on the VCR, and the account of what actually happened came across the screen.

Mizan's face was clear as day as he held up an unidentifiable man. The other figure's face could not be seen from the angle that the camera had recorded the scene. You could make out his clothing, but no facial figures. Alija's face also was clear as day as she peeked into the room. The jury sat back and watched as what had began as a robbery ended in a murder. Nancy Schwartz turned off the tape and watched the reaction that she got from the jury. They couldn't believe that all of this had been caught on candid tape, and that the man who had done it was still roaming free. "The young woman that you saw in that tape is willing to tell you what she saw that day. She fingered Mr. Williams. She called him out by name for the police. How can you deny that he is not the murderer?"

Carmen stood up as she watched the DA take her seat. "That tape proves nothing," she started out. "If anything it shows the type of person that Mizan Simmons was. He initiated the chain of events that night. He had a gun of his own, which he used to threaten the figure in that tape with. The face of the murderer is not even visible, and until you hear the witness testify, you should not let this tape affect your decision. It is weak evidence, circumstantial at best."

Carmen walked down the aisle and toward the door of the courtroom. She opened it up and in walked ten different men. They all had the same complexion as Kasheef, were the same height as him, and they all wore the same brand of designer jeans just off their waistline, and the same shirt that Kasheef had worn the night of the murder. "Judge these men from the neck down, which is the only part of the shooter that can be identified. Can you distinguish between them? The assailant had no identifiable scars or tattoos. Can you tell these men apart?" she asked persistently. "I can't. As a matter of fact, any one of these men can be the perpetrator."

Carmen could see the question marks going off inside

of the jurors' heads. That was all that she needed to do: create reasonable doubt. She turned toward the gentlemen who she had brought in and said, "Masks please."

Each man placed a black hood over their heads making their faces unidentifiable and their bodies identical. "As you can see, ladies and gentleman, there is no way to distinguish these men from one another without having a clear view of their faces. They all look like the murderer. It could be anyone."

Kasheef couldn't help the sly grin that crossed his face. Carmen was slick. She had game, and it was at that moment that he realized she was worth every single red cent that he was paying her. He was more confident than ever before. Carmen had just put a major dent in the prosecution's case. He already had Alija on his team, so all he had to do was let the case play out.

Kasheef barely listened for the remainder of the day. His mind kept drifting back to the night he had shared with Alija. Her smile, her eyes, her face were all embedded in his mind. He wondered why she had not shown up for his trial today. He didn't know that, after seeing her attend the court sessions, the prosecution had decided that it would be best if she stayed out of sight until it was her time to speak. They did not want her there until it was absolutely necessary. Silently, he wished he could see her face. Just the fact that she sat in the back of the courtroom gave him reassurance. He turned once more to make sure that he had not missed her, but she was nowhere to be found.

Norelle sat behind him, but only because she thought everything was good between them. She was a woman who presented herself under false pretenses. Her outward beauty was magnificent, but inward she was just as ugly as the grimiest niggas in New York. While stick up kids held men up with their guns, Norelle's weapon of choice was a combination of good looks and good pussy. Kasheef shook his head and turned back around just in time to hear the judge adjourn the trial for the day.

Kasheef stood and buttoned the top button of his coat. He leaned in and kissed Carmen professionally on the cheek and whispered, "Good job today, ma. Once this is over I owe you dinner a'somethin'."

"I eat lobster and steak," she replied with a smile. "Let's hope tomorrow is just as successful." She gathered her paper-work, walked out of the courtroom, and bypassed reporters as she hopped into the Lincoln Town Car that awaited her curb-side.

She headed toward her office. She had a lot of reading to do on other cases. Since taking on Kasheef as a client she had been neglecting her other responsibilities in the office. She knew that it was important for the senior board members of her firm to see her as well rounded, so she needed to balance all of her case trials successfully. With Alija on their team now, and the excellent cross-examinations she herself was presenting, she was confident that the win was in the bag. All of her hard work was paying off. She was finally moving up the corporate ladder. It did not bother her that she was riding Kasheef's criminal wave to the top. *As long as I get there,* she thought as she cruised the city streets. *I'll be the youngest senior partner and the first black woman to achieve that at the firm,* she thought proudly. Losing was not an option; she was determined to win . . . by any means necessary.

Chapter Thirteen

Alija sat at her baby's side. She was well enough to be off of the monitors, and Alija was relieved to finally see some progress in her daughter's health. She held Nahla on her lap as she sat in the rocking chair, flipping through a photo album.

"See, look," she cooed to her daughter and pointed at the pictures. "Here are you and Mommy." She turned the page. "Here you are, Mommy, and Daddy." A smile crossed her face as the pleasant memories from the photos flooded her memory. "And here you are again. You are Mommy's little angel, Nahla." She kissed her baby lovingly. "Mommy loves you."

"Hmm, hmm." Kasheef cleared his throat to announce his presence in the doorway. Alija turned toward him.

"Oh," she said in a surprised tone. She closed the photo album and slid it into Nahla's diaper bag. With her daughter still in her arms, she stood and looked at Kasheef awkwardly. "I did not know you were standing there."

"I wasn't. I just got here and I didn't want to startle you," he said. He moved closer to her and she took a step back. "I see Nahla's doing better." He held out his hands to the infant, and to Alija's astonishment, Nahla leaned toward Kasheef. She handed her daughter over to him and smiled.

"You might want to stop coming around so much. She is going to think you are her father. You already have half of the nurses thinking you are her daddy," Alija joked.

"Speaking of that . . . where is her father?" Kasheef asked. He knew that Alija had a past, but he wanted to know exactly what he might be getting himself involved in if he chose to pursue her seriously after the trial.

"Not that it's any of your business, but he ain't in the picture anymore," Alija said with one hand on her hip.

"I was looking for you today in court," he admitted. "I was hoping you would come." Nahla playfully touched his face as he talked, and he held her so intimately that someone would have thought that Nahla was his child.

Alija looked down at her feet nervously. "After last night . . . I just felt uncomfortable. I don't know. I just needed to think. Plus, the prosecution doesn't really want me there anyway. Witness intimidation, you know?"

"I intimidate you?" he asked sincerely.

"I don't know," she responded. "I just need time to think."

"About?" he asked.

"My life, the plans I have for her life," Alija said, pointing to Nahla.

"I was hoping you might make room for me in both of your lives," he said genuinely.

Alija's eyes met his and he reached out his free hand to pull her near. She resisted a little, but eventually stepped toward him. He wrapped his arm around her waist and kissed the top of her head. Closing her eyes, she inhaled the scent of his He cologne and put her hand on his chest.

"What am I doing?" she asked aloud.

"Letting me in," he replied. He looked at baby Nahla and smiled. "Ain't that right, ma?"

Nahla gurgled baby sounds and Kasheef said, "See she's feeling the kid."

Alija laughed and held onto him tightly. Just the sensation of a man's strong embrace made her feel safe. It was something that she had been missing. For a moment she had some security in her world and she desperately wanted to hold on to it. She finally noticed the gift bag that sat at his feet. "What's this?" she asked as she bent down to pick it up. She peered inside and found three Dora the Explorer children's books. "Thank you," she accepted graciously.

He sat down in the rocking chair, grabbed one of the books from Alija, then began to read to Nahla. Alija watched in amazement as Kasheef interacted tenderly with her daughter. Most men would run in the other direction if she told them that she had a child, but Kasheef seemed to be running toward her. They were developing the most intimate connection she had ever had with another person in her life. She was afraid; afraid that the actions she was taking would change her life forever. The two of them stayed by Nahla's side until she was fast asleep. After they put her back into the pediatric hospital bed, they walked out with Kasheef's arm draped around Alija's shoulders.

"Did you drive here?" he asked as they stepped onto the pavement of the parking lot.

"Nah, I took a cab. My car is bullshit. One day it works, the next day it doesn't," she said.

"You gon' have to cop you something new with all that cash you extorting from me," he said jokingly. She hit him on his shoulder and smirked in response. "Get in," he said as he opened his passenger door for her, and she looked around nervously.

"Kasheef, we can't be seen together," she whispered.

"We good, there ain't nobody out here. Besides my windows are tinted. Quit worrying," he assured her. She hopped into the truck and he closed her door before walking around to the driver's side.

When they pulled up to the hotel, Kasheef let her out at the entrance. "I'll meet you in my room in a couple minutes," he said while slipping her a key card to his room.

She got out of the car and walked into the lobby of the hotel. She could not help but feel as if her life had become one of those romance movies. She peered around to make sure there were no prying eyes around her. After taking the elevator to the twenty-first floor she had to take a couple deep breaths before she made her way down the hallway to Kasheef's room. Her nerves were making her feel as if she were going on her very first date. The flutters in her stomach felt more like eagle's wings than butterflies, causing her to feel faint.

When she walked into the room her eyes watered from the sight in front of her. "Oh my God," she whispered as she looked around her. There were candles and rose petals everywhere. An intimate indoor picnic for two was set up on the floor. Her heart raced. She was definitely in over her head. She was beginning to fall for Kasheef and he had made it perfectly clear how he felt for her. She didn't even realize he was in the room with her until his arms were wrapped around her waist.

"Why are you doing this?" she asked weakly as her eyes closed against her will. She enjoyed the feeling that his lips brought to her neck.

"I want you," he admitted. "I don't know what it is about you, Alija, but you were built for me, ma."

Alija turned to face him. "Kasheef, I have a daughter. I can't just start this with you as easily as another chick could. There are things that complicate this situation. All of my decisions affect her. I'm just trying to do right by her. I know what kind of lifestyle you lead. I saw you kill Mizan. Why would I want my daughter to be around that? I'm not even gon' front like I've always been responsible, but that night in the club you

forced me to change. Seeing him get shot right in front of me . . .
that changed my life, Kasheef . . . forever."

"I hear you, ma, but that still ain't telling me what I need
to know," he stated frankly. "I want to know if you can put all
that aside. I want to take care of you and Nahla. I would never
let anything happen to you."

Against her better judgment, she kissed his lips sensual-
ly. The chemistry between the two of them was insane. It literally
felt like sparks were flying throughout the room, and every single
spot of her body was sensitive to Kasheef's touch. "You've got
my heart, ma," he said with his forehead pressed against hers.
"I've never felt the things that I'm feeling for you."

"Where would we fit in your life, Kasheef?" she asked
with genuine concern and doubt.

"There's nothing but room in my world, ma. It's just
me. I'm all alone. I have been for a long time now. Things are
going to be a little crazy until this trial is over, but after that, my
life . . . our life together, will go back to normal," he guaranteed.

"I don't want to live in New York," she said.

"Then you don't have to. Whatever you want, Alija, I'll
give it to you," he promised.

"I don't know why, but I believe you would," she replied.

Kasheef pulled her down onto the floor where he pulled
out fresh fruits and wine for them to indulge in. It was the most
romantic thing that any man had ever arranged for her and Alija
was open. They sat up into the wee hours of the morning just
talking and laughing. They got to know each other a little better.
Kasheef noticed that it was five o'clock in the morning and he
yawned deeply.

"Yo', I ain't stayed up talking like this since I was in
middle school kicking whack game to the young girls on three
way," he stated with a chuckle.

"I know. It's easy to lose track of the time, though, when you're in good company like me," she bragged playfully. "You better get some sleep, though. You have court in just a few hours."

"Right now that ain't important," he whispered. "The only thing that matters right now is me and you."

Alija blushed as Kasheef massaged her feet. "Why me?" she asked.

"Why you what?"

"Why are you so interested in me?" she asked more clearly.

"You remind me of someone I used to know," he replied.

She frowned. She did not like being compared to some other girl. That meant that she was only a replica of the real thing he had lost. "So you really aren't feeling me. You just like me because I remind you of some other girl you used to love. What, she broke your heart and I'm her substitute?"

"You remind me of my mother . . . she passed away a couple, years ago," he said.

Alija immediately felt like an idiot for assuming the worst. She pulled her feet away from his grasp and quickly apologized. "I'm sorry."

"It a'ight, ma, you didn't know. There is just something in you. It's in your swag, like you're strong. You are a survivor. You out here trying to raise your daughter on your own . . . it's just a combination of things that remind me of her. She raised me by herself. I never knew my father. We were like our own team. A two-man show. We never had much, but we had each other and that was always enough. She was the only woman I have ever loved. I was protective of her. I would have done anything to save her. Nobody else just seemed to be able to compare," he explained.

"She sounds like a beautiful person, Kasheef," Alija admitted.

"I know. After she died I didn't think about her for a long time. It just hurt too much. It was so much easier for me to just shut off my heart than to deal with losing her. Now every time I look at you, I'm reminded of her."

"Is that a good thing?" she asked. "I don't want you to hurt every time you look at me."

"Nah, ma. It's the exact opposite. My heart seems to heal the more I'm around you."

"What are you saying, Kasheef?" she asked as tears filled her eyes.

"I'm not trying to scare you off, ma," he said. "But I care a lot about you."

"I care about you too," she replied with her head bowed in shame.

Kasheef frowned. "Why do you say it like it's a bad thing?"

"You could never understand. I don't even want to get into all of that. It's too late and I'm too tired," she said.

Kasheef pulled her body near his and grabbed the covers and pillow from the bed. He wrapped them over their bodies, and within moments they were both sound asleep.

The next day Alija awoke to the sound of a baby's laughter. She thought she was dreaming, but when she opened her eyes she saw Kasheef holding her daughter.

"Say hi to your moms, shorty," he said as he placed Nahla in Alija's arms. Alija looked up at him in shock.

"When did . . . how did you?" She was so stunned that she could not form any questions in her mind to ask.

"I talked to her doctors. They said that it was safe to bring her home. I knew you missed her, and since they thought I was her father anyway they allowed me to sign her discharge papers," Kasheef explained.

"Thank you, Sheef," she said, calling him by his nickname for the first time. Hearing her shorten his name let him know that she was becoming more comfortable in his presence, and he smiled.

"You're welcome," he answered. "Are you coming to the court house today?"

"Yeah, I'll be there," she replied. He fixed his tie and leaned in to kiss Alija on the lips.

"Bring baby girl, too; she might be my good luck charm," he said as he walked out of the room.

The trial went on for the next couple of days and Alija found herself sitting in the back row with her daughter faithfully. The district attorney pitched a fit about her being there, but she refused to leave. She told them that she wanted to face her attacker, when she really just wanted to show her support for Kasheef. After surprising her and bringing her daughter home early, Kasheef had claimed a tiny piece of Alija's heart. It was too hard to deny him, so she found herself giving in slowly, regretfully.

Kasheef was grateful for her support and was slowly but surely falling in love with this woman. They spent every day together. Alternating between his room and her room. She liked how he was so at ease with Nahla and she appreciated how he respected her as a woman, but more importantly as a mother. Alija was like a temporary vacation from life's everyday grind for Kasheef. She was who he talked to when he needed to get something off of his chest. She gave him peace of mind and her smile brightened up his day no matter how bleak it may have been. It got to the point where he honestly could not remember how he had ever been happy without a woman like her by his side. Even when they were not in each other's presence, she stayed on his mind and he carried her spirit in his heart. She was as close to perfect as someone could ever be, and once the trial was over he planned on showing her how much he appreciated having her in his life.

The most important day of the trial was approaching fast. The day that Alija was expected to take the stand was only a few days away and everyone was on edge. Everything was riding on her and she knew it. She was nervous; she did not want to mess up in any way. She had to speak her words as if she were telling the truth, and she figured the easiest lie was to say that Kasheef was not even at the club that night.

Kasheef still had some things to take care of. He contacted Carmen and asked her to set up a meeting with a federal prosecutor.

"Kasheef, I don't think it is wise for you to contact them in the middle of your case," she advised.

"There's just something that I need to handle, concerning the drugs that were found during my arrest," he responded.

"Kasheef, I really think you should wait until they bring those charges against you," Carmen said.

"Why haven't they indicted me yet?" Kasheef asked curiously, knowing that the fed boys didn't play. Going up against them your chances were slim, and he hoped to be in the wind by the time those charges came back up.

"They must be after someone bigger than you . . . maybe your supplier?" Carmen speculated. "Either way, if you go in there you are going to ruffle feathers."

"Just set up the meeting," he said before flipping his phone closed. He was eager to get this business with the feds handled. Even if he beat the murder there was a good chance that he would be convicted if he was prosecuted for the heroin charge. This is where the game got tricky for him. He had to play chess with his enemies and knock out two birds with one stone.

He had to be smart in how he moved. At this point, any wrong move could land him a permanent spot behind the bricks, and he dreaded that more than he dreaded his own death. Kasheef never wanted to put his life in jeopardy again, and since he planned on sharing his life with Alija, he knew that he would have to give up the drug game. He needed to make preparations to make a clean break so that his past could never come back to haunt him.

There was still the issue of Kasheef's connect. He would not want to see Kasheef's business go. Kasheef knew that he would have to have some type of incentive for Osti if he wanted to exit peacefully.

Kasheef went to a pay phone and contacted Osti to set up a meeting with one of his people who was already in the States. After that was done, he contacted Stick, who had been loyal to him for years.

"I need to get with you about something, fam," Kasheef said.

"A'ight, come through my spot," Stick responded. "Give me about an hour."

"A'ight, I'll be there in an hour. It's important so make sure you are alone," Kasheef instructed before snapping his phone closed.

Stick was only twenty-one, but was as thorough as most old heads in the game. Kasheef had found him when he was ten years old and was selling candy to people coming out of the grocery store in the middle of the summer. The young boy had caught his attention because Kasheef knew that schools did not do fundraisers during summer vacation, and he confronted the boy about it. A youthful Stick was honest, and when Kasheef asked him why he was posted in front of the store, Stick replied, "I'm just trying to get my shine up like you. I'm trying to eat."

Kasheef laughed at the boy and purchased his entire stash of candy bars. He rode by the same spot for a week straight and sure enough, Stick was posted in front of the store relentlessly, getting his hustle on. Kasheef respected the young boy's tenacity and grind. He immediately recognized him as good corner boy material and put Stick onto the game. Stick had moved up in the ranks quickly because he was smart and ruthless. If Kasheef was not going to be getting money anymore, he knew that there was no better person to pass his empire down to then Stick.

An hour and a half later, Kasheef pulled up to Stick's Crown Heights project building. He placed a call to Stick to let him know he was in front of his building. A couple minutes later, Stick came walking out of the building.

"What's good, fam? You sounded kind of urgent on the phone," Stick said. He stepped into the car and Kasheef pulled away from the curb.

"It's about time you came into your own, fam," Kasheef said as he whipped his Navigator through the hood. "I think you're ready. I've seen your ass grow up from a little, hardheaded mu'fucka to a grown man. Ain't no need for you to play the back no more. You were patient and you waited until your time came, fam. I appreciate that. Most of these mu'fuckas out here trying to take what they haven't earned. You have earned it though."

"Earned what? You speaking in circles," Stick replied.

"My spot. I'm retiring from the game. After the trial is over, I'm done. I've already set up a meeting for you to meet with my connect and everything," Kasheef said.

Kasheef reached out his hand and Stick shook it. "Yo', fam, good looking out, but there's only one problem."

"What's that?" Kasheef asked curiously.

"That new cat, Fiasco, is fucking up the game. I guess he's been moving weight out of the Bronx. He's been stepping on my toes lately. He is coming to our blocks shooting up shit, scaring our workers. He talking 'bout ain't nobody working them corners unless they slanging for him," Stick replied.

"Why am I just now hearing about this?" Kasheef asked harshly. "I knew the nigga was trying to make money and I didn't hate on that, but now this li'l mu'fucka getting out of hand. When niggas gon' learn to stay in they lane?" he asked heatedly.

"I didn't want to cloud your head. You know with the trial and everything I thought I should wait to let you know, but recently this mu'fucka been doing some real disrespectful shit. He's spitting venom on your name and everything. Mad niggas been jumping ship. They trying to be on the winning team, nah mean? I'ma ride with you until the end, fam, but you know when people think you down they automatically count you out."

"Yeah, bitch niggas always do switch sides, but your boy is far from out, fam," Kasheef assured him as he rubbed his neatly trimmed goatee.

"I told you before I've even seen your chick Norelle with him. At first they were real low key with it, but recently she's been riding shotgun with the nigga and everything. In the club on his arm and shit . . . just real disrespectful, nah mean?" Stick said.

"You have put in a lot of work for me over the years. It's your time. Don't no new mu'fuckas run New York, fam. That ain't happening. I'll take care of him, you just be ready to step into the big leagues. You're the boss now," Kasheef said.

Kasheef circled the block once more before pulling back up to Stick's building. "You got to come up and have a drink with your boy or something," Stick said. "I got to celebrate, fam."

Kasheef shook his head. "Maybe another time. I've got one more loose end I need to tie up," he said. He tossed Stick a cell phone. "This is how Osti will contact you. He's the only one who has that number. I don't even know it. He will call you when he's ready for you."

Stick nodded and shook hands with Kasheef once more before Kasheef pulled off. He retired to the hotel and found himself making his way to Alija's room. He knocked softly on her door. She answered it wearing a gold lace camisole and lace, boy-cut panties to match.

"Shh!" she whispered as she opened up her door and invited him. "I just put Nahla down. She was a little cranky today but . . . ." She stopped talking when she noticed the look on Kasheef's face. "What's wrong?" she asked.

Kasheef grabbed her arm and brought her near him. With his hand caressing the nape of her neck he kissed her slowly. "I love you."

The look on Alija's face was one of shock and panic. She did not know what to say. Here he was laying all of his cards out on the table and all she could do was stand in front of him, speechless. When her heart returned to a normal pace she took a deep breath and finally, unsurely replied, "I love you too, Kasheef."

He scooped her into his arms with ease. "I swear I'm gon' give you the world, ma. Just believe in me. Trust me. Be loyal to me and I will give you everything you need or want. If I can't give it to you then I'll die trying, I promise you that, ma."

Alija kissed his nose and replied, "I love you, Kasheef. I wasn't supposed to, but I do. I promise to give you everything that you deserve."

She got into her bed where Nahla lay peacefully. "Come lay with me," she said. Kasheef stripped down to his boxers and crawled underneath the covers. He took Nahla from the bed and lay her tiny body on his chest. Alija smiled and lay underneath his arm. "Good night, Kasheef."

He kissed the top of her head. "Get some rest, ma."

They both went to sleep knowing that they each held the other's future in their hands.

Chapter Fourteen

The morning of Alija's testimony came quickly, too soon for some, not fast enough for others. Kasheef and Alija moved around her hotel room silently. They both had burdensome thoughts on their mind, and the air between them seemed too thick to talk. Kasheef finished dressing and grabbed his keys. There was one more thing that he had to do. Before he left, he stood in front of Alija.

"How do you feel?" he asked her, concerned. He could see the stress taking over her face. She was usually so vibrant and relaxed, but today her features seemed to be set in a permanent scowl.

"Nervous," she answered truthfully. "And confused."

"I don't want to put any more pressure on you," Kasheef said. "I just want to let you know that I love you. I love you more than anyone in this world and no matter what happens today, that will never change, a'ight?"

Alija nodded and gave him a weak smile.

"What about Norelle? When she hears me—"

Kasheef placed a finger to Alija's lips. "Norelle is already taken care of. I got you ma, just trust me." He kissed her one last time. "I've got to go," he said. Alija nodded, but she could not help but feel like this was the last time she would ever see him. She felt like she was suffocating and all she wanted to do was run. Run away from her problems, run away from the confusing game that her life had become.

A half an hour later he stood in front of the federal building. He took a deep breath before stepping inside, knowing that
there was a possibility that they might not let him walk back out
with his freedom intact. It was a risk that he had to take. He took
the elevator to the eleventh floor where the Drug Enforcement
Agency was located. Confident in his Calvin Klein, two-piece
suit, he stepped up to the receptionist as if he belonged, with the
stride of a man on a mission. "I have information pertaining to
a heroin ring here in the city. I need to speak with someone in
charge," he said calmly.

In less than ten minutes flat he was sitting across from
Dan Greene, the chief of the DEA. "I hear you have some information regarding some illegal activities that are going on in the
city," the chief said as he stared intensely at Kasheef.

"Yes, I do."

"And why are you just volunteering this information?"
he asked suspiciously.

"I know you are aware of my arrest. I am going through
a very public trial right now," Kasheef stated.

"I know who you are, Mr. Williams," the chief responded. He leaned back in his leather chair and put his hands behind his head as he swiveled in his chair from side to side. He
squinted in suspicion and added, "The question is, what are you
doing in my office?"

"I'm here to help you help me. I'm sure you are aware
that when I was arrested, twenty kilos of heroin were found as
well. I didn't know that the drugs were in the house, but I know
who they belong to," Kasheef lied.

The chief pulled out a notebook and a pen then slid it
across the desk, his pale fat hand contrasting with the dark mahogany wood. "Start writing," he instructed.

In one swift motion, Kasheef tossed the pad right back

at him. He sat back in his seat and folded one leg across the other. "I'm not going to do your job for you. I just have some information that will lead you in the right direction. Norelle Gibson. That's whose apartment the drugs were found in. If you watch the company she keeps, you will find your source. Norelle helps him move his product up and down the East Coast. If you check her accounts you will uncover a gold mine." Kasheef stood up to leave, but turned to face the chief before exiting. "I trust that this will prevent DEA from opening a fresh case on me?" he asked, making sure that he had dotted all of his Is and crossed his Ts.

The chief nodded and replied, "If this leads pans out, then you have my word."

"I need better than your word. I need that told to my lawyer," Kasheef replied as he slid Carmen's business card across the desk. The man didn't like the fact that he was bargaining with a criminal but he made the call anyway.

Once everything was in place Kasheef went to leave.

"Oh, yeah, and good luck on that murder rap. We didn't need to open a fresh case on you for the drugs. You hung yourself when you killed that kid. You blacks get off on that . . . killing one another," the chief stated sarcastically as he picked up the phone.

That's what you think, Kasheef thought with a smirk. The chief did not know it yet, but he was going to have the last laugh when it was all said and done.

***

Norelle stepped out of Fiasco's BMW and kissed him gently before walking into the courthouse. Today was the day that she would receive her emancipation. She was getting ready to hear the testimony that was sure to set her free. She walked through the crowded building eagerly, hoping to run into Alija before the day's proceedings began. She saw her being escorted out of the DAs office.

"Alija!" she called out as she maneuvered her way in and out of the crowd. Alija stopped walking and turned to see who had called her name. The DA waited and watched the interaction so that she could see who was interacting with her star witness. She did not need anyone throwing a wrench in the plan. Alija was due to testify that day and she did not want any interruptions.

"I'll be right back," Alija told Nancy Schwartz as she made her way over to Norelle, looking her up and down as she approached. She couldn't help but turn up her nose at the woman. *How stupid can she be to give up a man like Kasheef? He would have taken care of her if she had just stuck by him.*

"I just wanted to make sure our agreement was still intact," Norelle said discreetly as she stood in front of Alija.

"Everything is going to go as planned," she assured her. She turned and walked away to rejoin the DA. Butterflies filled her stomach as she was placed in a small holding room until it was time for her to enter the courtroom. The state had arranged for Nahla to be taken to a daycare so that Alija could be present in court. She took several deep breaths as she paced around the small office. She hoped that nothing went wrong. She desperately needed for things to go right. The contents of her stomach sent a wave of nausea through her body and she gasped for air. She was so overwhelmed that she could not hold her breakfast. She rushed to the bathroom and barely made it as she vomited in the toilet. She heaved violently until nothing else would come up. She splashed cold water onto her face. *Calm down,* she told herself. It felt as if the room were spinning and she hoped that her nerves would settle before she was due to speak. She sat down and closed her eyes before sending a silent prayer up to

God. She was going to need all the help that she could get to pull this off.

***

"The state of New York calls Alija Bell to the stand," the district attorney announced. The large wooden door creaked open as Alija appeared. Kasheef's heart melted when he saw her. Her skin glowed as if she had been personally kissed by the sun, and her honey brown complexion complimented the cream H&M dress she wore. A large gold belt was wrapped around her tiny waist, and her feet were blessed with gold, strappy stilettos. The way that her hair was pulled up away from her face allowed Kasheef to take in all of her features. At that moment he knew exactly why he loved her so much. She was his idea of perfection. She was his love. Her heels clicked against the floor as she glided up the aisle and into the witness chair.

"Raise your right hand and place your left hand on this Bible," the bailiff instructed. Alija inhaled deeply and did as she was told. She glanced over at the jury and Mickie gave her a discreet wink of reassurance.

"Do you swear to tell the truth, the entire truth, and nothing but the truth, so help you God?"

"I do," she responded.

The judge looked at her and said, "Thank you, Ms. Bell, you may be seated."

Alija's breath caught in her throat as her nerves took over. She could feel the stares penetrating her as she watched the DA approach.

"Ms. Bell, can you tell us where you were and what you saw the night of March 21, 2008? Please don't leave out any detail. Take us through that night as you can recall it."

"I was at Club Blaze with some friends. I was with Mizan Simmons, having a drink at his booth," she began. She glanced at Kasheef, who was staring at her intensely. His facial expression was calm. He trusted her completely to deliver her testimony just as they had rehearsed.

The DA noticed her hesitate and urged her on. "Please, continue, Ms. Bell."

"I was having a couple of drinks with Mizan Simmons and the club began to let out. I was a little drunk. I had been drinking all night. All of my friends had already left the club, so I got up to leave too. I was halfway to my car when I realized that I had left my purse and keys inside of the club at the table that I was sitting at. I went back in to get my stuff. The club was empty, but there was light on upstairs and I could hear voices." Alija's eyes began to water and she closed them as tears began to cascade down her face.

Norelle listened intently as she waited for Alija to ID Kasheef. She bit her nail anxiously and tapped her foot nervously. She was anxious for the trial's conclusion and could not wait to move on with her life.

Kasheef's heart broke in two as he watched Alija relive that night. The tears on her face caused knots of guilt to form in his stomach. The love that he felt for Alija was unmatched by any emotion he had ever felt before. He just wanted to protect her. He wanted to be there for Alija and Nahla. He never wanted to be the cause of her pain again. He looked over at Carmen, who returned his gaze.

"Is all of this a part of the plan or is she going to turn on us?" Carmen asked in a furtive whisper.

"We don't have to worry about her," he reassured her.

"Now, what were these voices saying?" the DA grilled.

"I don't know," Alija responded as she opened her eyes and caught Kasheef's gaze. "I can't remember."

"You can't remember?" the DA asked as she gave Alija a look that sent chills up her spine.

"No, I'm sorry, I cannot recall what they were saying," Alija responded.

The DA stalked over to her desk and flipped through her notes. "Okay, Ms. Bell, well, what did you see?"

"I walked in and I saw two men. They were yelling at one another. Mizan had a gun, but the other guy pulled his gun as a reaction and shot Mizan. I ran after that. I did not see what happened next."

"And is the man you saw shoot Mizan Simmons in the courtroom today?" The DA asked.

Alija paused before answering. She looked at the jury and stopped at Mickie, who nodded slightly, urging her on. The courtroom was so still that you could hear the faint sound of Norelle's heel impatiently tapping against the floor. Alija felt herself gasping for air as she tried to calm herself down.

What the fuck is she doing? Norelle thought as she set her sweating palms on her skirt and rubbed feverishly in anticipation.

"No," she finally answered.

No! I know this bitch is not trying to cross me. I paid her $75,000! Norelle was livid as she stood. Before she could open her mouth to speak, the door of the courtroom opened loudly as four suited gentlemen walked in. Kasheef turned around in his seat and watched the scene play out.

"Norelle Gibson?" one of the gentlemen asked.

"Order in this courtroom!" the judge yelled as he banged his gavel and the crowd whispered in speculation.

"Yeah?" Norelle responded unsurely. "Who are you?"

"My name is Agent Greene and I'm the chief of operations for the United States Drug Enforcement Agency," he stated.

"And? What the fuck does that have to do with me?" she asked indignantly.

"You are under arrest for the distribution of heroin and tax evasion," he said as he turned her around and began to apply handcuffs to her small wrists.

"What! Wait, you are making a mistake!" she screamed.

"No, ma'am this is no mistake. Pretty girls like you make me sick. You're almost worse than the drug dealers we lock up because they get involved with that life to chase tail like you. Now, you have the right to remain silent . . ." The agent continued to read Norelle her rights, but she didn't hear one word. She gave Kasheef a pleading look, but the malice that she found in his gaze told her that he had set her up. They pulled Norelle out of the courtroom kicking and screaming.

Bang! Bang! "Order in my courtroom!" the judge yelled as he hit his gavel against his desk.

Carmen looked at Kasheef in disbelief. "Is that what you had me set a meeting up with them for?"

"Just do your job, ma. If you want to represent your girl after my case is over then be my guest, but it was either her or me. The bitch tried to pay Alija to testify against me. She wanted me to get this time so that she could spend my dough. She had it coming to her," he whispered and then refocused his attention toward the front.

Carmen could not believe what had just happened. She knew that she could not help Norelle right now. She had to finish her job and represent Kasheef. She shook her head in blatant disgust at him as she mumbled, "Unbelievable."

"Believe it," he whispered back.

The judge slammed his gavel several times to regain control of the room. Once everyone was silent, the trial resumed. Kasheef winked at Alija as she continued. "I don't see Mizan's shooter in the courtroom."

A look of irritation spread all over the DAs face as she persistently continued to steer her witness back into the right direction, "But, Ms. Bell, did you not tell a Detective Nielson of the NYPD, and I quote, 'Kasheef did it. I'll testify to protect my daughter,' end quote?"

"I did tell the detective that I would testify in order to protect my daughter, but he is the one who brought up Kasheef Williams's name. I had never heard of him before I was arrested. He is not the man I saw," she said confidently.

The DA walked back to her chair, her frustration and exasperation made clear when she flopped down in her chair and put her hand on the side of her face while in deep thought. This was Carmen's cue to spring into action. "Your Honor, it is obvious that the state has done everything in their power to falsely convict my client. I would like to move for immediate dismissal!"

The judge looked toward the DA. "Mrs. Schwartz, do the people have any other evidence against Kasheef Williams?"

Nancy Schwartz's face was flushed and red in anger. Holding back her emotions, she stood and replied, "Your Honor, even without Ms. Bell's testimony we have provided evidence against Mr. Williams. I think that it is only fair that we proceed with this case and let the jury decide."

The judge nodded. "I agree. The trial will continue, but we will adjourn for the day. Closing arguments will resume tomorrow, after which the jury will deliver their verdict."

Alija stepped down from the witness stand, and if looks could kill she would have fallen dead where she stood and been circled in chalk as hard as the DA was staring. She walked out of the courtroom, relieved that her ordeal was over. She had done all that she could for Kasheef. Now all she could do was wait.

Kasheef left the courtroom with a huge smile on his face. Alija had pulled it off and her tears had only intensified the effect of the false statement she had given. He was sure that the jury had believed her. As he walked through the courthouse he felt rejuvenated and confident for the first time since the trial had begun. Alija was worth every penny he had agreed to pay her. He felt forever indebted to her. The performance she had put on was sure to get him off. He exited the courthouse and descended the steps, then got inside the limo that was waiting for him curbside. He went straight to his accountant's office to retrieve the remainder of Alija's money. He could not wait to see her and share his future with her.

"Are you sure you want to do this?" His accountant asked skeptically. He had witnessed Kasheef's grind over the years and he knew how long it had taken him to accumulate his wealth. "This is a lot of money. You have worked very hard for this."

Kasheef nodded and replied, "I'm positive. I'm going to marry this girl. She just saved my life today. I trust her."

His accountant nodded and handed Kasheef paperwork to sign. Kasheef signed it without reservations. The accountant made him copies and put them inside of the suitcase that contained Alija's money.

Kasheef couldn't wait to see Alija. When he arrived at the hotel he went to Alija's room. Before he could even knock on the door Alija opened it with a smile on her face. "I was waiting for you," she said. He scooped her into his arms excitedly and kissed all over her face.

"Aghh!" she screamed playfully and laughed giddily as he spun her around in his arms.

"I love you, girl," he told her as he set her down on her feet. "Where's Nahla?" he asked.

"She's still at the daycare. I figured I would pick her up in a couple of hours," she replied.

"Here, sit down, I need to talk to you," Kasheef stated seriously as he pulled a chair out for Alija. He put the briefcase on top of the small eating table and popped it open. "Here is the rest of the money that I promised you."

Alija smiled and ran her hand over the neatly arranged bills. The amount of money was overwhelming, and she had to stop herself from screaming she was so happy. Even after she paid Mickie $50,000 for all of her help she would still have more than enough money to live comfortably and give Nahla the best of everything.

Kasheef removed two pieces of paper and handed them to Alija. "Read these," he instructed.

Alija began to scan the document. "Aloud," he said gently. Alija frowned and looked up from the paperwork.

"What is this about, Kasheef?" she asked.

"Just read it, ma. It's important."

Alija sighed. "I, Kasheef Williams, hereby give Alija Bell joint ownership of Cayman Island account 5487624008630 and Swiss account 74639957203. There is a combined amount of $2,500,000 in these accounts." Alija stopped reading the document and stared at Kasheef in disbelief. "Kasheef, I can't accept this. This is too much," she objected.

"I want you to have that, Alija. I'll give you all that I have in order to keep you." Kasheef stood in front of her and got down on one knee. "I need you, ma. I know this is all happening kind of fast, but I know this is right. You are right for me, Alija. I love you. You are the only person that I have loved besides my mother in my entire life. Will you be my wife?" The three-karat, platinum, princess-cut ring was blinding.

Alija closed her eyes. She could not believe what was happening to her. She could not breathe and she gripped Kasheef's hand tightly. *I'm not supposed to be in love with him*, she thought frantically. She felt his hand grace her cheek and before she could come to her senses she responded, "Yes. Yes, Kasheef, I will marry you."

Chapter Fifteen

Alija sat nervously in the back of the courtroom as she waited for the jury to come back with a verdict. She stared at her engagement ring and her stomach filled with knots. She wished that she could have talked to Mickie before the deliberations began, but it was too late. Whatever was going to happen was already in motion. There was no turning back now.

Kasheef's heart felt as if it would explode as he sat in the federal courtroom. News cameras were littered throughout while both supporters and the opposition awaited the verdict. It was the day that he would meet his fate, the day that the rest of his days would be determined by the decision that the jury rendered. On the outside Kasheef was calm and collected. His chocolate Armani suit rested perfectly against his dark skin and medium athletic build. With his hair cut neatly in a fresh Caesar and his eyes filled with sincerity, one would never guess that the man sitting before them was a drug kingpin. Kasheef scanned the jury with his eyes and couldn't read their expressions. He didn't know what tomorrow held for him and for the first time in his life he was afraid. Prison was not an option for him. To lock him up would be equivalent to stealing his pride, and he refused to live on his knees. Kasheef hoped and prayed that the verdict would be delivered in his favor, because if it wasn't he was already prepared to go out in a blaze of glory. A $10,000 cash payment to one of the assigned court officers ensured that he would have his weapon of choice, a chrome .45, taped underneath the defense table. He discreetly ran his hand along the underside of the cherry wood and felt the cold steel that was strapped securely in place. It was his insurance policy.

Kasheef was not green to the game. He had been in the dope game since he was a young boy, so he knew that his day of judgment was inevitable. While many glamorized the street life, he knew the real deal and was well aware that his reign could end in only one of two ways: prison or death. He would much rather hold court in the streets for his actions, in his own environment, where he would at least have a chance to survive. Sitting in a courtroom made him a sitting duck. He knew that it was very possible that the jury would convict him, and that the judge would throw the book at him, sending him away for the remainder of his life. He turned and stared into the eyes of Norelle, his girlfriend who greeted him with a wink and a sexy smirk. Cameras flashed continuously in her face, but she took it all in stride. She knew that they had recognized her face from her very public arrest that had occurred the day before. She didn't care however; she had just come to see what the verdict would be for Kasheef. From her Manolo stilettos to her Marc Jacob, two-piece suit with matching clutch, she represented all that he was. He was a miracle worker and had taken her from the gutter and put her in a throne beside his own as the queen of the streets. She held her title well, no matter the cost and indeed she commanded attention like royalty. *You didn't think I would come,* she mouthed as she discreetly stuck up her middle finger. Kasheef knew that she would be out on bail, but he was confident that the feds would have enough evidence against Norelle to convict her. He looked past her and Alija's face stuck out from the crowd. She gave him a weak smile and he nodded to acknowledge her. He couldn't show it, but his heart warmed at the simple gesture that Alija had given him. Just the simple things that she did made him happy. He was glad that he had her support.

"All rise!" the bailiff announced loudly, causing Kasheef to turn back around in his chair. "The honorable Judge Campbell Martin presiding."

"Be seated," the judge mumbled as he took his own behind the large pedestal. "Has the jury reached a decision?"

The face of the foreman told Kasheef all that he needed to know. Kasheef gripped the steel underneath the table and took a deep breath as he prepared himself for what was about to go down.

"Yes, we have, Your Honor."

"And what say you?" the judge inquired.

"We the jury . . ."

Kasheef's hand wrapped tightly around the gun. The anticipation made him sweat slightly as he closed his eyes and waited to hear if he would walk out a free man, or leave in society's constraints.

"Find the defendant . . ."

His heart beat in his ears, blocking out all sound as he watched the foreman's lips mouth the words.

Pow! Pow! Pow!

The verdict fell on deaf ears as the courtroom erupted in mayhem. Norelle grabbed one of the court officer's 9 mm pistols and fired as many shots as she could get off. With rage in her eyes and her finger around the trigger, she went after Kasheef with a vengeance.

"No!" Alija screamed as she ran toward the front of the room. The guards drew their weapons and surrounded Norelle.

"Get down! Now, put down the gun!" they yelled. Norelle didn't comply, but instead raised her gun to finish off Kasheef who was gasping to fill his lungs with air and squirming from the hot lead that had entered his body. It was only the bullet that pierced her heart that managed to stop Norelle's relentless, burning rage, and her body instantly went limp as it fell to the ground. Her head hit the floor with a hard thud and she lay motionless next to Kasheef, who was writhing in agony.

Alija tried to run past the groups of people who were gathered around Kasheef, but the officers stopped her. "Move! Let me go! Don't touch me!" she yelled as she struggled to get past the crowd. "Please! I need to make sure he's okay." No matter how much she fought they would not let her through. The area was quickly secured and stretchers brought into the courtroom to take Kasheef and Norelle to a hospital.

Everyone was confused and stunned by Alija's reaction to Kasheef's shooting. When Kasheef reached out his hand for her and whispered, "I love you," the press went wild. Carmen and Alija locked eyes, but Alija quickly stormed off, headed for her car.

Carmen turned toward the judge. "Your Honor, the verdict?"

The judge shook his head and replied, "The jury found him guilty."

"What?" she asked incredulously. *There has to be some type of mistake*, she thought. *Alija's testimony should have been enough to free him.* She looked around at the disheveled courtroom and the blood splattered on the floor. She turned around and found her boss standing near the exit, shaking his head. His thin lips were clamped together and she could tell he was fuming. *My career is over.* The entire case had exploded in her face and crumbled at her feet. She walked right past him without speaking. She had to finish her job and tell her client that she had lost the case and that he would be going to prison . . . if he lived to see another day. She fully intended on filing an appeal, but if she had lost the first case there was no guarantee that she could win the next, and at that moment Kasheef was loss to the state.

Chapter Sixteen

Eight weeks passed before Kasheef was able to stand before the judge for his sentencing. Alija had stayed by his side the entire time he was recuperating in the hospital, and he was saddened that their time together was being cut short. She sat directly behind him with her daughter in her arms. She cooed and reached for Kasheef while tears fell freely from Alija's eyes. She had been so confused during the entire trial. Now that it was over, her heart ached and she felt as if her best friend was being taken away from her. Carmen sat by Kasheef's side as they awaited the judge's decision.

"Mr. Williams," the judge began. "You have been found guilty by a jury of your peers for second degree murder. Does counsel have any recommendations for sentencing?"

"Your Honor, the state would like to request that Kasheef Williams be punished to the fullest extent that the law allows," the DA said.

"Your Honor, my client has been unjustly found guilty of a crime that he did not commit. I would like to state for the record that we will be filing for immediate appeal, and I ask the court to show restraint on Mr. Williams in regards to his sentencing," Carmen stated.

The judge removed his glasses and said, "Mr. Williams, I hereby sentence you to no less than fifteen and no more than twenty-five years in Sing Sing Correctional Facility. You will be remanded into immediate custody."

"Kasheef?" Alija cried. "I'm so sorry, Kasheef," she said as she stood to hug him. He reached for her and she held him tightly. "I'm sorry, Kasheef."

"It's all right, ma. What are you sorry for? You've done nothing but make my life better. Listen to me, Alija," he said sternly as he blinked away tears. He knew that he had to remain strong. "I'm gon' be okay. You take that money and you look out for yourself, a'ight? Come see me sometime. I love you. You're the only woman I've ever loved, remember that."

The guards took Kasheef away and Alija stayed inside the courtroom until she could no longer see his face. With each step that he took, a piece of her left with him, and the onslaught of emotions was almost unbearable as she held onto Nahla, the only constant in her ever-changing life. She felt like there was a revolving door where people constantly entered and exited her heart, leaving her to mend the broken pieces after they were gone. She kissed her daughter and hugged her tightly. "It's all over, Nahla. It's all over."

***

"Williams, you have a visitor," the CO yelled as he unlocked Kasheef's cell. Kasheef stood. It had been three months since he'd been sentenced and only one person had visited him so far: Stick. He had communicated with Alija through letters only. He had asked her not to come and visit him because he did not want her to see him locked behind bars, in his weakest state, and chained like an animal. He sauntered to the visiting area, his feet shackled, and his pride wounded.

"Table four," the CO told him. Kasheef approached the table and was surprised to see Alija sitting before him. She had put on a little bit of weight, but it was all in the right places, and just her presence seemed to lift a huge burden from his shoulders.

"Hello, Kasheef," she said with a half smile. He could

tell her spirit had been dampened by his imprisonment, and the sparkle that she had when they first got to know each other was dim. The fact that he could not be with her killed him. Alija held Nahla in her arms, and Kasheef noticed that the baby had grown tremendously in the short time that he had been absent from her life.

"I miss you, ma," he said, his voice heavy with built-up emotion as he put his hand against the glass that separated them.

"I miss you too, Kasheef," she whispered as she matched her hand alongside his. She stared at his face, taking in every single feature. Her heart fluttered at the sight of him before her and she instantly knew how they had come to be so close. At first, she couldn't understand how she had let herself fall so hard. Kasheef was a forbidden love. She experienced something with him that she had never felt before. In many ways, he was her man. Ironically, he was the only man that she had ever fully trusted. "I can't stay long. I just came to give you something." Her voice broke up as if she was ready to break down, but she quickly cleared her throat and willed her emotions away.

She handed a manila envelope to the guard who was monitoring their visit, and he inspected it briefly before passing it to Kasheef. Kasheef opened the folder and pulled out the first piece of paper. It was an ultrasound picture. His eyes shot up from the photo to Alija's. He stared at her more carefully and noticed the small bulge in her stomach. She was pregnant. He closed his eyes and had to stop the tears from forming behind his lids. Alija was pregnant with his first child, his only child, and here he was stuck in prison unable to give her the support that she needed. He would never be able to be a part of his baby's life. He gripped the phone tightly and took a deep breath before he opened his eyes. "You're pregnant with my seed, yo'?"

Tears built in Alija's eyes when she heard the sound of

his voice. He was holding back his cries, but she could hear the undeniable sadness that was threatening to pour out of him.

"I'm sorry, Alija," he said sincerely.

"No, I'm sorry, Kasheef," she replied as she wiped away a tear that escaped her eye. "There's more."

Kasheef removed a set of photos. He flipped through the photographs slowly, one by one. There was a picture of Alija. He smiled, knowing that this would help him make it through a lot of days. Just having an image of her face would make the time go by easier.

"You're beautiful," he complimented her. He went on to the next picture, a picture of Alija and Nahla. He loved Nahla. She was a miniature version of her mother, and he silently hoped that Alija was pregnant with his son. A girl and a boy would make their family complete. He pulled out the next photograph, a picture of Alija when she was pregnant with Nahla. He flipped and it was a more recent picture of Alija. He peered closely at it. "Are you pregnant with my baby in this photo?"

She nodded and gave him a half-hearted smile as he flipped to the last photo. When the image registered to his brain, he dropped the pictures onto the steel table as if they were as hot as fire. He couldn't believe his eyes. He turned the picture over to make sure he wasn't seeing things and he noticed the inscription that Alija had written on the back.

Kasheef,

I told you from the beginning that it would be so wrong for me to love you. I don't know how I let myself fall for you, but now you know why we can never be. This is exactly what you deserve.

He turned the picture back over, his hands shaking. He stared closely.

Alija, Nahla, and Mizan smiled like the happy family that they were before Kasheef ruined their lives. Mizan was Nahla's father and Alija's lover.

"You killed my baby's father, Kasheef," Alija finally admitted. The tension that she had carried on her shoulders since the day Mizan died finally lifted from her, and it was as if a weight had been removed from her heart.

"What?" Kasheef asked as his eyes met hers, desperately searching for answers. He shook his head, unwilling to accept the naked truth as it had been lay out in front of him.

"We were supposed to get married and make a life together after he was released from jail," she said through her tears, her voice heavy with sorrow. "I begged him not to get back in the game but he wouldn't listen. He said that he was doing it for us, so that he could take care of his daughter. You killed Nahla's father, and I had to make you pay for what you took from me; for what you took from Nahla. I didn't mean to fall in love with you. That wasn't a part of the plan. I just wanted to put you away so that my daughter and I would be safe, but you got to me. You got inside my head. You offered to take care of me and you gave me what I needed to take care of my daughter. You gave me all of your money to start a new life, and you gave me your heart. It was so tempting to take, Kasheef, but I couldn't forget that it was because of you that my life was in shambles in the first place. That is why you're here. For revenge," she said as she wiped her eyes and willed herself to stop crying. "Even though I love you, you have to pay for what you did to him."

He stared up at Alija as she arose from the table. He was speechless. He watched her walk over to another girl who had been sitting in the waiting area. His eyes bugged in disbelief as he recognized the girl from his trial. She sat in on his jury. *Alija set me up. All along she set me up*, he thought as his heart dropped into his stomach. He felt sick and his eyes burned, but he held back his emotions. It was hard for him to believe that everything that he had shared with her had been a lie. She had seemed so sincere. Her love had seemed so real. He had thought that they were so official. She was the closest he had ever been to true love and now he was finding out that it was all a lie. *This shit can't be true.*

"Alija!" he called for her as he stood and watched her walk away. He was not willing to let her leave just like that. He had to know more. He had to keep her in his life for as long as he possibly could. It was as if the beat of his heart was dependent on her loving him. If she stopped, he was almost positive that his heart would too. He was beyond the point of self-preservation. Almost from the first moment he sought her out, they had become connected. He felt it and refused to believe that it had meant nothing to her. "Alija, please don't take my baby away! Don't do this to me!"

He was conflicted. A part of him was enraged and hated her for being able to penetrate his shell. She was his weakness and he resented her for making him vulnerable. Because of her, he was susceptible to pain, but the other part of him could not possibly hate the woman who was carrying his seed; the woman who had cracked his hard exterior and gotten him to love. She was the woman whose smile could brighten his darkest hour. She was his salvation and with her love he could make it through the hell he had been reprimanded to. "Alija!"

Alija halted mid-step. The sound of his voice caused her to close her eyes. She took a deep breath and returned to the table. She picked up the phone.

"What, Kasheef? Don't you hate me now? Haven't you had enough?" She waited for him to respond, but he was silent. She could see his broken spirit as she stared into the windows of his soul. "Huh? Why do you still want me? You can't love me now, because I hate you for doing this to me! Do you hear me? I hate you," she whispered vehemently.

"Don't say that, ma," he begged, his tears finally falling from his eyes. "I can't hate you Alija. I've never loved anyone the way that I love you. You put me in here, fuck it. I killed Mizan, but you saw what went down. You know how it happened. I'm not a murderer, Alija. You know me. I was protecting myself. I did what I had to do, you know that. I love you, ma. Don't take my child away from me. Don't leave me in here on stuck."

Alija was bawling as she listened to him. Her heart ached because she really had fallen for Kasheef. In another lifetime he would have been her man and possibly her husband. He would have been her king, the one she shared her hopes and dreams with, but in this lifetime they could never coexist.

Kasheef could see the wheels turning in her head. "Tell me you don't love me, ma. You can't tell me that Mizan meant more to you than me. You love me, Alija. I can see that shit in your eyes," he said passionately, with fire in his gaze and through clenched teeth.

Alija stared him directly in the eye. "How can I raise Nahla next to her sister or brother and tell her that you are the one who killed her father? How fair is that to her? I can't let her see me love you and think that it's okay, Kasheef. It's not okay. It was wrong for me to let it go this far. It doesn't matter how I feel about you. I have to think about my children. Mizan may not have meant more to me, but he meant more to Nahla. That's my daughter, I have to protect her." She touched her stomach and finished, "I have to take care of both of them."

"They're my shorties too, ma. I'm in love with your baby girl just as much as I love you. And the one that's growing inside you *is* me, Alija. That's my seed, yo'. Don't do this to me," he pleaded.

"You did this to yourself," she said. "Good-bye."

All this time, Kasheef thought as he put his head in his hands in despair. *She had someone working on the jury to sway them into a guilty verdict while she worked me to sway me into giving her my cash.* He looked down at the ultrasound and let his emotions flow without restraint. A combination of feelings raced through him. Rage. Respect. Love. Hate. He felt them all for Alija at that moment. She was the woman he had fallen in love with; the one he would have given his life for without regret. *She is the mother of my child, yo',* he thought numbly. His heart ached in a way that he had not felt since the death of his mother. Alija was his everything and she had just walked on his heart with her Manolo stilettos. All he had wanted was her love and loyalty, but she was in fact loyal. Loyal to her man. The only problem was that her man was Mizan.

Kasheef stood up and punched the glass with all his might, struggling to let go of some of his rage. He returned to his cell. It was the place he would call home for the next fifteen years, courtesy of Alija Bell. *I guess Mizan really did get the last laugh. The nigga reached out from the grave to get his revenge.* He taped the ultrasound to his wall. He told himself that he would look at them every day and ask God to bless the child that he would never get a chance to meet. The ultrasound was the only piece of his family that he had left, and he prayed that one day the emptiness he felt inside could be filled by the return of the love of his life. Until then, his fate was sealed behind the steel and concrete that made up the desolate prison. Pain was love, and it was the story of his life.

Coming Soon

Excerpt from Noah AJ Wright's next novel

GOON

Chapter One

"A toast to the good life," Dayvid Porter said as he raised his glass while sitting at the head of the long oak table, accompanied by his three sisters. They were in a safe house on the outskirts of suburban Baltimore. They had just accomplished what so many before them had failed to do. They were about to retire at the top of the game as career criminals. The diamonds from their last heist were scattered over the table and over three million dollars sat in the corner of the room in six large leather duffle bags. Everyone raised their glasses to join in the toast that Dayvid had proposed. As Dayvid looked around the table, he smiled. He, along with his siblings, were about to leave the country as winners. They had terrorized the state of Maryland for the past five years and their names rang a bell in the streets. Ruthless was an understatement if describing the Porters. They hit over fifty-five banks and jeweler spots and never once got caught. They had also murder-for-hire and had a 100 percent success rate in that department. Robbing unsuspecting hustlers wasn't beneath them, either. They loved to catch the new up-and-coming street king and take him for everything he had. Selling drugs wasn't their thing. Their logic was, "Why waste time hustling and stacking money when you could wait for another man to do it for you . . . and then rob him?"

***

Meet Autumn:

Autumn was the youngest of the family and at age twenty-two she was a seasoned veteran. She was the perfect bait for a gullible hustler because of her attractive features. She stood five foot five, thick, and as feisty as they come. She had a caramel complexion and was very street savvy. She had a habit of wearing green contacts, which only added to her natural beauty. All the dope boys wanted her and all of the hood chicks hated her. You would have a better chance catching a faithful Muslim eating a pork sandwich while having a ménage á trois with two white girls before you would see Autumn without designer clothes and shoes on. Needless to say, she was a fashion junkie. Born and raised in Baltimore, Maryland, she was schooled to be a hard knock and as thorough as any street nigga bred there. Autumn acted as the getaway driver for bank jobs because Rain didn't feel she was ready to go inside the jobs yet.

Meet Fallon:

Fallon was heavy set, chocolate, and the loud one of the bunch. She loved to get the drama popping and had a murder fetish. Her perfectly wrapped hair and smooth skin was attractive to most men. But relationships never lasted once men found how dominating she was. She was known to trick on niggas just to get her nut off, then it was out the door they went. For lack of better words, Fallon was a real bitch and was nymphomaniac. Also a stone-cold killer, never afraid to take a life or go out in the blaze of glory.

Meet Dayvid and Rain:

Dayvid was the only male and was the oldest, along with his twin sister Rain. He stood six feet tall with a solid frame. His high yellow complexion made him the lightest of the bunch. He was the heart and soul of the vicious crew. Acting as the protector of his sisters, with a tattooed tear on his face and a fully covered tattooed neck, gave him a grimy look.

Rain was the brains of the operation and the oldest, coming out of their mother's womb two minutes before Dayvid. She was tall, slender, and yellow. Her long hair was always braided to the back and she shared the same tattooed tear on her face, just as her brother did. Although Rain was a woman, she had no attraction to men whatsoever. She had never made love to a man and didn't plan on doing so. She was born a woman, but everything about her screamed "hood nigga." She was soft-spoken but hands down the most cold-hearted of the Porters. She was the one who planned the robberies from top to bottom. Rain was known in the streets the most, with her having connections with the top hustlers and baddest females. Rain was one of a kind. People don't get built like her often. She was quiet, loyal, and brilliant. Most definitely the street's favorite.

They drank champagne and celebrated their last night in B-more. It was a long time coming, and finally they were about to relocate and start a new, crime-free life in the Cayman Islands. They all had their passports and fake IDs ready to go and by the same time the next day, they would be in Saint Tropez relaxing on a yacht somewhere, with no worries in the world.

Rain downed the last of her drink and got up as everyone sat around the table talking shit about how they were about to ball out on the islands.

"Yo', I got to go and hit Smitty off before we leave," Rain said as she picked up her gun off the table and put it onto her waist. She was referring to the inside source they had. Smitty was a middle-aged man who was a friend of their deceased Nanny. He put them up on all the capers, bank robberies and diamond heist. He also acted as their consultant and advisor, being that he was an ex- criminal who was known for being one of the best bank robbers Maryland had seen during the 80s.

"Damn, you didn't handle that earlier?" Dayvid asked just before he took another gulp of the expensive drink.

"No, I got too busy. I was trying to get to the safe house and I forgot to stop by his place." Rain walked over to the smallest bag that contained close to one hundred thousand dollars in it, and threw it over her shoulders.

"Yo', you want me to roll with you?" Dayvid asked, but Rain rejected, knowing that she was going to stop by and see her girlfriend, Laura, before she returned. She had to tell her goodbye before they left Maryland for good.

"Nah, I'm good. Y'all do y'all thing and I will be back later. Save me some of that champagne, too, nigga," Rain said as she headed out the back door to hop in her tinted Monte Carlo. She had a fleet of cars, but liked to stay low key and not stick out. Her Monte was always her preferred car when she wasn't trying to stunt, staying under the radar.

Rain cruised down the street, while the sounds of the rap group Mob Deep bumped lightly out of the sub woofers in the back. Rain slowly bobbed her head and let the blunt hang from her mouth as the highway almost put her in trance. She was in her own world, reciting every lyric to the song. She approached Smitty's exit and veered off.

Rain pulled into the driveway of a nice-sized house, which was in a pleasant and quiet neighborhood. Smitty met her at the door with his signature straw hat and as always he had a toothpick hanging from the left side of his mouth.

"Rain, come in," Smitty said as he let her in. "Have a seat," Smitty offered as he sat down on his large-sized sectional couch that sat in the middle of his spacious living room. The big screen was displaying the NBA playoff game.

"Thanks," Rain said as she flopped down on the sofa. "Here you go," she murmured, tossing the bag onto Smitty's lap.

"My girl," he said as his eyes instantly went to the bag as he opened it up to find rubber banded, one hundred dollar bills.

"So this is it, huh? The last score," he said as he tossed the bag behind the couch, knowing that he didn't have to count it.

"Yeah, we are out of here first thing in the morning." Rain said as she slowly nodded and rubbed her hands together.

"You guys had a good run," Smitty said as he glanced at the television and then back at Rain.

"Yeah, it was fun," Rain answered, thinking about all of the heists they pulled off. The adrenaline rush that robbing gave her was like no other. It was a thrill that only one of her own kind could fathom. The excitement of watching tellers stuff money into a bag got her off. Also, the fact that they never stayed in a bank or diamond spot for more than ninety seconds was a rush that not even a drug could match. Rain, along with her siblings, was addicted. But all good things come to an end and their end was on that day.

"Rachel would have been proud of you guys," Smitty said referring to the woman who raised them all, who was also their auntie. She passed about ten years back, but her legacy lived on through the Porters.

"Yeah, she would have."

Rachel, aka Nanny, had adopted the four kids after their parents were killed in a car accident. Rain and Dayvid were only ten and had to grow up quicker than their peers. Rachel was a well-known booster and kleptomaniac, so by default, she taught them how to utilize their five-finger discounts. Little did she know, she was feeding the flames of something much bigger. She made them the outlaws that they grew up to be and their childhood acted as their training period.

"I'm going to miss having you guys around," Smitty said as he looked at the woman who sat in front of him. He knew her since she was a young buck and always knew she was the most intelligent of the crew.

"We're going to miss you too," Rain added as she stood up, and so did Smitty. "I'm about to go 'head and take off. See ya' around," Rain said, not wanting to say good-bye.

"See you around, kiddo," Smitty said as he embraced her. Rain walked out of the door and knew it probably would be the last time she saw Smitty again. "I will always be here if you need me," Smitty added, letting her know that he was their backbone.

"I know," Rain answered as she got in her car and headed over to Laura's house. The next good-bye wouldn't be so easy. Laura was her love and she had to break the news to her that she would never see her again. Rain purposely waited until the last possible moment to let Laura know that she was leaving, so she couldn't try to protest. In Rain's eyes, it was better that way.

***

"Oh God!" Laura moaned as she was on all fours, buck-naked in her bed. Rain sucked on Laura's pussy from the back, while digging her nose into Laura's other hole. Laura rubbed her own breast as she was in total bliss. Before Rain she had never been with a woman, but there was something about Rain's swagger that had her open. Laura's plump, oversized cheeks wiggled in the air as Rain put her tongue to work, moving it rapidly on Laura's clitoris. Slurping sounds filled the air as Laura began to thrust her ass against Rain's face, dripping her juices onto her bed sheets.

"I'm about to cum!" Laura announced as she felt her

body begin to tremble and her legs become wobbly. Laura squeezed her own breast even harder as she felt her love coming down. Rain quickly left Laura's clitoris and stuck her tongue in her other hole, completely driving Laura crazy. Without hesitation, Laura began squirting all over her bed as her legs gave out on her, landing her flat on her stomach, shaking like a fiend craving for a hit. Rain smiled as she looked down at Laura, watching her have an orgasm for a couple of seconds. Rain lay down next to her with a sports bra and a pair of boxers on, as she began to stroke Laura's hair.

"I love you, Rain Porter," Laura said as she breathed heavily trying to catch her breath. Rain ran her fingers through Laura's long hair. Laura was half Cuban, half black, and had olive-colored skin with a head full of soft curly hair that enticed her gorgeous appearance.

"I love you too, ma. We have to talk about something," Rain said as she held Laura in her arms.

"Oh, shit. What is it now? I know that tone all too well," Laura said while smiling and rubbing Rain's flat stomach. "You're leaving town for a couple of days or something?"

"Something like that," Rain answered, not knowing how to tell Laura that it would be the last time she would ever see her.

"What is that supposed to mean, Rain?"

"It means that I am going to be away for a while," Rain said feeling the tension grow. Rain knew that Laura was feisty and would pitch a fit if she told her the entire truth, so Rain just wanted to give her false hope to avoid the drama.

"You always do this!" Laura yelled as she sat up and crossed her arms tightly across her chest. "I'm tired of this fly-by-night shit. You always come through, eat my pussy, and then leave like a thief in the night. I love you, Rain, and I need you around." Rain didn't know to respond to Laura. Rain knew that she was right and that made it much harder for her to tell her the truth. Rain leaned over and grabbed Laura's face, kissing her gently and slowly.

"I love you, ma. I am going to come back for you . . . I promise," Rain regretfully lied as she hugged her and embraced her for over a minute. Rain jumped up, knowing that she had to get back to her brothers and sisters so they could finish tying up loose ends before fleeing.

"I will be waiting," Laura said as she got up and hugged Rain once again. By the way Laura hugged her, it was as if she knew that she wouldn't see Rain again. Rain breathed deeply and got one more whiff of Laura's always-fresh body scent and kissed her on the cheek.

Rain put back on her pants and reached into her pocket pulling out a roll of money that added up to just under twenty thousand dollars. She tossed it on Laura's dresser and just like that, she was gone. She left Laura naked and alone in the bed with a broken heart.

Rain headed back to the safe house with Laura on her mind. Fuck that, Rain thought as she tried to shake off her sad feeling knowing that love could get you killed. The life she led was dangerous and love had to no place in her existence. She had to be cold-hearted without ties. That was the only way she knew how to be. The only people she needed was her family; anything or anybody else was a potential problem.

As Rain pulled onto the street of the safe house, her heart dropped. She saw flashing lights and men with ATF jackets with guns crawling all over their house. Her heart skipped when she saw three officers escort Dayvid out of the house, handcuffed with a blunt dangling from his mouth.

"No, no, no," Rain said repeatedly as she hit her steering wheel with force. The nosey neighbors stood outside in their robes and pajamas while forming at circle as they witnessed the spectacle happening on their block. Rain slowly rode past and saw her other two sisters get escorted out also. Fallon saw Rain slowly rolling by and quickly looked away, not wanting to tip the police off. The looks in Fallon's eyes were as if she was telling Rain to go as far away from the scene as possible. Rain took the unsaid advice and slowly pulled off. A tear dropped from her eye as she hopped on the freeway, heading to Smitty's house to figure out what was the next move.

Chapter Two

Rain's heartbeat was rapid as panic set into her soul. This had not been in their plans. They were so close to getting away from this lifestyle. Since their childhood they had been hustlers. They were bred to rob and steal. Nights of endless plotting, gruesome capers, and getting money were all they knew. They had planned their escape down to the last little detail and on the eve of their departure their world had come crashing down around them. Her brother and two sisters were all that she had. Seeing them taken into federal custody was one big reality check. "Fuck!" she yelled as she hit the steering wheel. She was overwhelmed as emotions swelled around in her chest. *How did we not know we were on their scope?* She fumbled with her cell phone as she dialed Smitty's number. If anybody could give her answers she knew that he could. As she whipped through Baltimore City streets she frantically dialed his number.

"Come on, Smitty . . . answer the phone," she urged as she checked her rearview mirror in paranoia. She peered cautiously at every vehicle that got behind her, fearing that it may be her turn to be arrested next. She was not naïve and knew that if the FBI had gotten involved then they were under surveillance for a while. *They probably know everything,* she thought as slammed her phone shut after being sent to voice mail.

As she thought of the feds she quickly rolled down her window and tossed the phone out. *We were careful . . . every time*

I made sure everyone followed the same routine. If they knew where to find us, the feds were probably tapping our phone calls, Rain thought as she pulled over at a shopping center to use a pay phone. She had to get back out to Jessup County, but there was no way she was rolling through the pay tolls. She was far from dumb and she knew that by now every cop in the city would be looking for her. She scrambled for spare change in her car and put the hood of her cashmere sweater over her head. She held her head down to conceal her identity as she rushed over to the pay phone. "Come on, ma . . . answer the phone," she urged as she shifted nervously from foot to foot, keeping her eyes on her surroundings. She kept her hand tucked inside of her leather Prada biker's jacket so that she had easy access to her burner. There was no way she was going down without a fight, and if the feds thought they were going to catch her slipping they had another thing coming.

"Hello?"

When Rain heard Laura's voice she sighed in relief.

"Yo', Lo, I need you to come get me, ma . . . like right now," she stated urgently, her tone almost desperate.

Laura knew Rain like the back of her hand and she had never seen her even blink in the face of danger; but the sound of Rain's voice alarmed her. "Where are you?" she asked without hesitation. It was the only question she needed to ask. She did not need details. All she knew was that Rain needed her. Nothing more needed to be said.

"I'm in the parking lot at Mondawmin Mall. Hurry up, ma, I need your help," Rain admitted before hanging up the phone.

Rain stood hidden inside the mall. She was so paranoid that she didn't even want to wait inside of her car in fear that the police would know what type of vehicle she was in. She had to keep her wits and play it safe if she wanted to remain a free woman. She checked her Movado watch as impatience caused her to pace back and forth. *Fuck is taking her so long,* she thought as her eyes anxiously examined every shopper that passed by. Finally she saw Laura's black Honda pull into the lot. She walked outside and hopped directly into her back seat.

"Pull off," Rain instructed as she ducked low in the seat.

"What's going on?" she asked. "Is somebody after you?" Laura asked nervously as she pulled away slowly while looking at Rain through the rearview mirror.

"Keep your eyes on the road," Rain stated nervously. "Just drive."

"What about your car?" Laura asked.

"I'ma need your whip and I'll leave my keys with you so you can come back to drive mine. First I need you to drive me out to Jessup," Rain stated. She was used to being in control and was giving out demands so quickly that she had forgotten to fill Laura in on what was going on.

"Wait a minute, lady . . . slow down. What the hell are you running from?" Laura asked.

"The feds . . . they've got everybody but me. I'm the last one standing and now I need your help so that I can get them back."

***

Rain sat hidden in the trunk of the car as Laura sat in idle traffic on the toll bridge. She could see the flashing police lights ahead.

"They're looking inside every car," Laura stated. "But they're not opening the trunk so we should be okay." Her rattling voice revealed her fear and her stomach felt hollow, as if she would throw up at any moment. She did not know what she had gotten herself into, but she loved Rain and would do anything in order to play her position.

"Just be cool and stop moving your lips. They'll wonder who you're talking to," Rain stated as she eased her head back into the trunk and sealed the back row of seats so that she could not be seen. She closed her eyes as the car moved slowly through traffic and she gripped her gun tightly, preparing herself for the worst. She had to make it to Smitty's house or she could kiss her family and possibly her freedom good-bye.

Laura's hands were a sweaty mess as she held onto the steering wheel with a vice grip. She was nervous and was no good at playing it cool. There were only two cars that separated her from the police barricades and she took deep breaths to try and calm down.

Just be easy, she coached herself as she pulled up to the small station. She reached into her purse and pulled out some money to pay the toll.

"Please move forward for inspection," the woman stated routinely.

Laura drove until the police stopped her. They gave her car one good once over and peered into her back seat before ushering her along.

"Whew," she blew out as she made her escape. She was almost positive that she would be busted. She got the hell out of dodge and when she was out of sight she said, "Okay, you're good."

Rain emerged from the back seat of the car and huffed loudly as she straightened out her wrinkled clothes. "Pull over," she instructed.

Laura pulled into a gas station and Rain got out of the car. She pulled a knot of money from her loose-fitting jeans and peeled off five hundred-dollar bills.

"I want you to take this and catch a cab back to my car," Rain stated. "You don't need to be involved in this any further."

Laura shook her head defiantly as her eyes watered. She had a bad feeling in the pit of her stomach that things were only going to get worse from here.

"No, Rain, I want to help you," she said.

"You did, ma," Rain replied. "But there is nothing more that you can do. If anybody comes to talk to you, you haven't heard from me."

Rain got into the car as Laura stared sadly at her. "Be careful, Rain," Laura pleaded. She leaned down into the window and kissed Rain's lips softly, then watched her pull away.

*****

As Rain pulled onto Smitty's suburban street, she circled the block cautiously to make sure that the coast was clear.

She rang the doorbell furiously until finally Smitty opened the door. When he saw her, he pulled her inside quickly then stuck his head out to make sure that she was not bringing heat to his doorstep.

"They're locked up . . . The feds came out of nowhere and arrested Dayvid, Autumn, and Fallon," she stated.

"I know," Smitty replied calmly.

"You know?" Rain replied loudly. "What the fuck is going on? How did we get caught up like this?" she asked rhetorically.

Smitty poured himself a glass of cognac and sipped it slowly before he led her into his study. He held the glass in his hand and pointed out his pinky toward the TV. "Every cop in the state is looking for you," he stated. Rain's mouth dropped when she saw her juvenile mugshot pop up on the screen as the news reports filled the TV with stories of her family's arrest.

She stared at the screen in disbelief as she watched a playback of the feds storming into her home and taking her brother and sisters away. "How did this happen? We were careful . . . we were supposed to be on our way to the Cayman Islands," she whispered.

"Somebody got sloppy. You all got too relaxed . . . too comfortable with your routine."

Her legs felt weak and she took a seat in the chair across from Smitty's mahogany desk. "You have to fix this, Smitty. You have to help me," she said.

"Ain't no helping them, Rain. Dayvid, Autumn, and Fallon are in federal custody. If these were local cops I would be able to pull some strings, but the feds are not letting this go. All of those banks that you were hitting over the years were federally-insured banks, Rain. You were playing with federal dollars."

"I remember you getting a cut of that federal money too," she stated defensively. "Where was all this apprehension then?"

"Look, Rain, I'm on your side. I know I played my part in this fiasco, but I covered my trail, too. I'm just trying to make sure you realize what you're up against. On top of the robberies there were also twelve bodies left behind," Smitty stated. "Your best bet is to get out of town. There is no way around this. This shit is going to end bad for everybody."

"There has to be a way!" she yelled. "I'm not leaving this city without them," she stated. "I know I'm asking you to go out on a limb for me, but please . . . I need to get them out of there. Maryland is a death penalty state, Smitty. We both know that if they stand trial they're going to lose, and with all of the murders we've committed . . . ."

Rain's words stopped in her throat as she thought about the fate that lay ahead for her siblings. "Fuck that . . . if we got to die it's not gon' be like that. We'd rather go out blazing," Rain said.

"It's going to take a whole lot more than a shootout to get them out of this," Smitty stated.

"Then tell me what it's gonna take," Rain replied. "After this we won't ask you for anything else . . . but I need you to call in one last favor."

Smitty could see the conviction in Rain's eyes as she pleaded with him on behalf of her siblings. He knew that whether he helped her or not she was going to try to break her people out of jail. He knew that it was how she was raised. He had known her since she was a little foster child growing up in the system, and the woman who had taken them in was a dear friend of his. She had taught them all of their klepto ways and had taught them that all they had in the world was each other. Their loyalty to one another was the only thing that was guaranteed.

Smitty sighed as he nodded and sat back in his seat.

"Okay . . . I'll help you. I'll make some calls and see where they are holding them. This is a long shot, Rain. You're only one person . . . they'll have twenty men guarding them," he stated, trying to reason with her.

Rain felt her adrenaline pumping from the fear of the unknown. She knew that she was outnumbered. Without her family it was her against the world. She sat back, stared him directly in the eyes, and replied, "Then I guess I'm going to need a lot of bullets to even things out."

Chapter Three

Rain leaned against the tall columns of the courthouse. She was completely inconspicuous and had changed her appearance so drastically that she was positive that her own sisters and brother would not recognize her. Her normal boyish clothes were replaced with a feminine, high-waist pencil skirt that hugged her curvaceous shape, and the ruffled blouse she wore even showed cleavage. Her usual pleated cornrows had been undone, and her hair flowed down her back in loose curls as she hid her face under a large, black sun hat. Shades covered her eyes and as she sat observing the surroundings of the courthouse. No one had the slightest idea who she was. She was America's Most Wanted and was sitting right in the pit of the fire.

As she held a cigarette between her fingers, she clutched a large, black Gucci bag in her hand. She was ready to get it popping. There were only two ways that the situation could play out: in glory or gunfire. She was prepared for both. The media was all over the place as everyone anxiously anticipated the arrival of the Porter trio. Rain's anger rose as she watched the commissioner of the police force brag about the arrest. His showboating sickened her and she smirked in amusement because she knew that his celebration would be short lived.

She noticed the city paddy wagon turn the corner of Calvert Street and she began to descend the steps slowly. Her breath caught in her throat as she made eye contact with her youngest sister. Autumn sat straight up in her seat and turned her head as she looked Rain directly in the eyes. Rain noticed the worried look on her sister's face and nodded in reassurance. *How many cops?* she asked in sign language. She was thankful for the little bit that she had learned from her deaf aunt. It was the first time that the skill had come in handy, and she needed it now more than ever.

Autumn turned her head to count the guards and then signed back, *three.* Rain nodded, and then looked around to count the amount of guards lingering outside near the press conference. All of the odds were against her, but she was going all out. She reached into her purse as she walked toward the front of the courthouse, where the police wagon had stopped. She made sure that she was far enough away. She held onto the small automatic machine gun in her hand, fingering the trigger, ready to pop anything in a uniform that stood in her way.

***

Autumn looked out of the window at her sister nervously and frowned. *What the fuck is she doing? She's so stupid . . . she should have left town.* Autumn turned and kept her eyes on her sister as the bus passed her. *Is that bitch wearing heels?* She took in Rain's odd appearance. Her leg bounced as nervous energy traveled up her spine. She could not sit still as she thought about going to stand in front of a judge . . . more than likely an old, white man. *He can't judge me . . . There is no way he could possibly understand everything we've been through that made us like this.*

"Will you stop doing that? You're making me fucking nervous," the girl chained to her stated in irritation.

Autumn moved her mouth to respond but she was tuned out when the loud blast erupted from the front of the carriage.

Boom!

***

As soon as Rain heard the explosion, she pulled her MAC-10 from her purse and popped off as she ran toward the burning vehicle.

Chaos erupted as bystanders ran for cover and the law enforcement on the scene ran toward the blaze. Only the front of the vehicle had exploded, killing the escorting officers instantly. Inmates emerged from the car in frenzy as they each took advantage of the blaze in an attempt to escape.

"Rain!" Autumn screamed from the window as she saw her sister spraying at the policemen. Her bullets laying them down one by one.

"Bitch, get your ass off the bus . . . and let's go!" Rain yelled without looking as she continued to shoot wildly toward the courthouse steps.

Autumn sprang to her feet and the girl beside her shook her head in protest. "Look I'm only here on a shoplifting charge. I'm not trying to—"

"Get up!" Autumn demanded as she stood up and practically dragged the girl against her will. Rain reached into her bag with one hand while firing with the other. She retrieved a 9 mm and handed it off to Autumn, who, without hesitation, trained it on the officers at the top of the courthouse steps.

"Where is Dayvid and Fallon?" Rain yelled as she frantically searched the crowd of fleeing inmates.

"I don't know. They separated us right after the arrest," Autumn screamed over the thunderous roars of her cannon as she shot at the police.

Rain's heart dropped when she heard the news, because she knew that it would be impossible to free Fallon and Dayvid.

"Look, just shoot the cuffs off of me and I'll take off . . . ." the girl screamed desperately, not wanting to be involved in what the two sisters in front of her had planned.

Knowing there was no time to separate Autumn from

the other inmate, Rain grabbed Autumn's hand and they took off running, with the girl protesting beside them. She had no choice but to run along to avoid the bullets that were flying around her head.

Rain felt the dead weight of the girl as she was trying to stop them from running, and she grabbed her forcefully by the arm. "Bitch, if you don't move your fucking feet!" she yelled in anger. They hopped into Laura's car and skirted off.

"A clip!" Autumn yelled when she realized she was out of ammunition. "I need another clip!"

"Look in the bag," Rain stated as she floored the car. She ran directly into a parked car and forced it out of her way as Autumn rummaged through Rain's bag and retrieved another clip. She popped it in and stuck her gun out of the window. She fired without hesitation as Rain drove them away to safety.

The further Rain drove, the less gunfire they heard. "Am I clear?" she asked as she switched lanes, cutting off another car. She hit a quick right, causing the car to tip on to two wheels.

"Yeah, you're good," Autumn stated. She leaned into the front seat with tears in her eyes and hugged her sister. "Whoo! I love your fucking ass!" she screamed as she thought of how close she had come to judgment day.

"Yeah, yeah . . . I love you too, bitch, now sit back and help me think about how to spring Dayvid and Fallon. They were supposed to be in that fucking transport van. Damn!"

The other inmate cleared her throat, "Look, I'm not trying to fuck up what y'all got going on, but can we figure out how to get these cuffs off so I can do me? No offense, but I'm not trying to be a part of what y'all got going on," she stated seriously.

"Ugh . . . can I smack the shit out of this whiny-ass bitch?" Autumn asked.

"Autumn, calm down . . . we will figure out how to get

the bracelets off, but nobody's going anywhere right now," Rain stated harshly as she stared at the girl through her rearview mirror.

The girl leaned her head back on the head rest. "Fuck . . . it had to be me," she mumbled. Rain drove to the outskirts of the city and headed to the first motel that she saw.

"Stay in the car," she stated. "I'm going to go get us a room."

"What if somebody notices you?" Autumn asked.

"They won't," she stated as she got out of the car. The pencil skirt and high heels were so uncharacteristic of Rain that Autumn had to make light of the situation. She stuck her head out of the car and whistled, giving her a catcall. "Work it, bitch."

Rain stuck up her middle finger. Autumn burst into laughter as Rain stormed into the office.

Fifteen minutes later they were all cooped up in the motel room as Rain paced back and forth, constantly peeking out of the curtains to make sure that they had not been followed.

"I can't believe this shit," the girl stated. "Hello, the handcuffs," she reminded them.

Rain stopped mid-step and looked at the girl like she was crazy. "How the fuck am I supposed to take them off, huh? You want me to shoot them off?" Rain asked sarcastically. "The gunshot would make too much noise and every fucking cop this side of Maryland would be beating down the door. So just sit back, shut the *fuck* up, and let me think."

"We have to go back for them," Rain stated after a few minutes.

"How? We can't just go in there like cowboys," Autumn stated. "You should have seen where they had me locked down at, Rain. There were armed federal agents at every door. There is no way the two of us are going to be able to pull this off. Not twice. Now that you busted me out they will be on their shit. They probably aren't even holding Day and Fallon in the same facility anymore."

"We can't just leave them," Rain whispered.

"I know, but we have to be smart. We can't win a war with the feds, so we have to outthink them," Autumn replied.

The girl scoffed as she shook her head.

"What the fuck is so funny?" Rain asked as she stared down the brown-skinned girl. Her Chinese eyes slanted in disbelief.

"This shit is unreal . . . that's what's funny," she spat. "Do you really think that you can save whoever you're trying to get to from out of federal custody? Y'all bitches are delusional." She began to laugh as she shook her head in dismay.

"You know what?" Autumn shouted, growing frustrated from the girl's pessimism.

"She's right," Rain said regretfully.

"She's not right . . . Fuck her!" Autumn shouted defiantly, hearing the hesitation in her sister's voice.

Rain let her head rest on the window pane as she closed her eyes. "We all knew the risk of what we were doing."

"You broke me out, Rain . . . you know the code. It's all of us or none of us," Autumn said passionately.

"Well, right now it's half of us, Autumn. We have to let things die down. Every man with a badge in this city is going to shoot first and ask questions later. We have to keep moving and get out of here while we still have a chance."

Tears accumulated in Autumn's eyes as she thought of abandoning Dayvid and Fallon. "What about Smitty? He can help us," she said, grasping at straws.

"He helped me get you. He already put his neck on the line for us. He made it crystal clear that it was the last time I needed to contact him," Rain informed.

Autumn's heart broke in two. As the youngest of her four siblings she was used to them taking care of her. Ever since she could remember they had protected her. They were always there for one another. Now she felt like a traitor. Their world had been rocked. Their King made checkmate.

"It wasn't supposed to happen like this," she said glumly.

"I know, but it did," Rain stated as she wiped a stray tear from her cheek. She inhaled deeply and put on a brave front. Crying wasn't going to solve their problems. She had never been soft and decided that there was no point of boo-hooing over spilled milk. *What's done is done.* "Get some rest," she stated. She looked at the clock and saw that it was ten o'clock in the morning. "We will sleep for a couple hours and leave when we wake up. We can't stay in the same spot for too long."

"Leave to where?" Autumn asked. "We don't have any money. The feds took everything."

"Then we'll have to do what we have to do to make our ends meet. We'll drive to Mexico. Once we cross the border, the feds can't touch us."

"Whoa!" the random girl stated. "I'm not going anywhere. Fuck that. Just let me go about my way."

"What's your name?" Rain asked the girl.

"Erin," she replied.

"Erin, as soon as we are someplace where we can fire a gun without making a scene I'll take the handcuffs off. Then you can go about your way," Rain replied.

ORDER FORM
URBAN BOOKS, LLC
78 E. Industry Ct
Deer Park, NY 11729

Name: (please print):_____

Address: _____

City/State: _____

Zip: _____

QTY	TITLES	PRICE
	16 ½ On The Block	$14.95
	16 On The Block	$14.95
	Betrayal	$14.95
	Both Sides Of The Fence	$14.95
	Cheesecake And Teardrops	$14.95
	Denim Diaries	$14.95
	Happily Ever Now	$14.95
	Hell Has No Fury	$14.95
	If It Isn't love	$14.95
	Last Breath	$14.95
	Loving Dasia	$14.95
	Say It Ain't So	$14.95

Shipping and Handling - add $3.50 for 1st book then $1.75 for each additional book.

Please send a check payable to:

Urban Books, LLC

Please allow 4 - 6 weeks for delivery

ORDER FORM
URBAN BOOKS, LLC
78 E. Industry Ct
Deer Park, NY 11729

Name: (please print):_____

Address: _____

City/State: _____

Zip: _____

QTY	TITLES	PRICE
	The Cartel	$14.95
	The Cartel#2	$14.95
	The Dopeman's Wife	$14.95
	The Prada Plan	$14.95
	Gunz And Roses	$14.95
	Snow White	$14.95
	A Pimp's Life	$14.95
	Hush	$14.95
	Little Black Girl Lost 1	$14.95
	Little Black Girl Lost 2	$14.95
	Little Black Girl Lost 3	$14.95
	Little Black Girl Lost 4	$14.95

Shipping and Handling - add $3.50 for 1st book then $1.75 for each additional book.
Please send a check payable to:
Urban Books, LLC
Please allow 4 - 6 weeks for delivery

ORDER FORM
URBAN BOOKS, LLC
78 E. Industry Ct
Deer Park, NY 11729

Name: (please print):_____

Address: _____

City/State: _____

Zip: _____

QTY	TITLES	PRICE
	A Man's Worth	$14.95
	Abundant Rain	$14.95
	Battle Of Jericho	$14.95
	By The Grace Of God	$14.95
	Dance Into Destiny	$14.95
	Divorcing The Devil	$14.95
	Forsaken	$14.95
	Grace And Mercy	$14.95
	Guilty & Not Guilty Of Love	$14.95
	His Woman, His Wife His Widow	$14.95
	Illusion	$14.95
	The LoveChild	$14.95

Shipping and Handling - add $3.50 for 1st book then $1.75 for each additional book.

Please send a check payable to:

Urban Books, LLC

Please allow 4 - 6 weeks for delivery

Notes